I0588373

Return to Morro Harbor

Alicia Gael

Other Bella Books by Alicia Gael

Murder on Castaway Island
Murder, Mayhem and Sex on the Beach

Praise for the works of Alicia Gael

Murder on Castaway Island

I didn't count how many times I had to remind myself to breathe. I was on the edge of my seat almost from page one and only sat back comfortably after I'd read the last sentence.

-NetGalley, Jude S.

This is like a modern day Agatha Christie. A well written fast paced, engaging and entertaining mystery. This will have you guessing who did it until the end. Well done Alicia Gael.

-NetGalley, Bonnie K.

This book had a bit of everything! It had suspense, action packed, intrigue, mystery, murder, revenge, a great who done it, great plot twist, and some crazy twists and turns! I definitely recommend reading this book as it was well worth reading!

-NetGalley, Debbie B.

Murder, Mayhem and Sex on the Beach

Murder, Mayhem and Sex on the Beach is a delightfully humorous rollercoaster of fun and flirtation wrapped around a good dose of suspense as the two main characters try to apprehend wayward probationers and take down the bad guys. The title sums the situation up perfectly.

-goodreads, Fiona S.

There is humor throughout, with witty dialogue and funny little jokes springing up unexpectedly. I quite enjoyed reading this book and look forward to more from the author.

-TheLesbianReview.com

Ms Gael has given us a fun, fast paced book that you will have to see for yourself. Great read.

-goodreads, Bee S

About the Author

Alicia Gael (she/her) has a Creative Writing Certificate from UC San Diego Extension, a master's in criminology and is a graduate of the Golden Crown Literary Society's Writing Academy 1-3. She is also a retired probation officer and criminal justice professor. Her debut novel, *Murder on Castaway Island* was released in January 2024 and received very positive reviews. Her second novel, *Murder, Mayhem and Sex on the Beach* was released in January 2025, also receiving positive reviews. Her short stories have been published in *The Bangalore Review* ("Deception") and *The Quiet Reader* ("No Time for Stories"). The first chapter of her yet-to-be-completed historical fiction novel, *The Journey*, was published in the 2022 CA Writer's Literary Review anthology.

When not writing, you'll find her reading, kayaking, and drinking prosecco. She lives near the California central coast with her wife, Donna.

You can contact Alicia on her website: www.aliciagael.com
Facebook: aliciagaelwrites
Instagram: aliciagael_writes
Bluesky: aliciagael.bsky.social
Email: aliciagaelwrites@gmail.com

Return to
Morro
Harbor

Alicia Gael

BELLA
BOOKS

Copyright © 2025 by Alicia Gael

Bella Books, Inc.
P.O. Box 10543
Tallahassee, FL 32302

All rights reserved. No part of this book may be used or reproduced or transmitted in any form or manner or by any means, electronic or mechanical, including photocopying, or for the purpose of training artificial intelligence technologies or systems without permission in writing from the publisher.

This is a work of fiction. Names, characters, businesses, places, events and incidents are either the products of the author's imagination or used in a fictitious manner. Any resemblance to actual persons, living or dead, or actual events is purely coincidental. The publisher does not have any control over and does not assume any responsibility for author or third-party websites or their content.

First Edition - 2025

Editor: Cath Walker
Cover Designer: SJ Hardy
Cover photo credit: A.G. Crumpler

ISBN: 978-1-64247-682-8

PUBLISHER'S NOTE

The scanning, uploading, and distribution of this book via the Internet or via any other means without the permission of the publisher is illegal and punishable by law. Please purchase only authorized print or electronic editions, and do not participate in or encourage electronic piracy of copyrighted materials. Your support of the author's rights is appreciated.

Acknowledgements

It takes a village to write and publish a novel, and this one is no exception. *Return to Morro Harbor* would never have seen the light of day without the help and kindness of so many people. First off, my beta readers: Susanne A, Erin P, Toni O, Margarete M, Cat B, Kim CG, and Donna B, I hope you know how much I appreciate the time and effort you put in to helping make this a better book. I'm forever in your debt.

Special thanks to Jen Lyon for being a good sport and agreeing to make a guest appearance in Morro Harbor.

My editor, Cath Walker. You didn't take it easy on me, and as a result this is a much better book than it would have been otherwise. Thank you.

Linda and Jessica Hill for taking a chance on me and giving me the opportunity of a lifetime. Everyone at Bella Books who had a hand in getting *Return to Morro Harbor* to the finish line. I'm eternally grateful for all that you do.

And of course, my wife, Donna, who pushes me when I need to be pushed, and takes away my phone when I should be writing. This one's for you.

CHAPTER ONE

Pulling off Highway 1, Devin Davis turned into the Harbor Beach parking lot and into a space facing the water. Lowering the windows, she turned off the engine and leaned her head back. Closing her eyes, she inhaled deeply, filling her lungs with salty ocean air. The familiar scent was calming after the four-hour drive. Exhaling slowly, she opened her eyes. The view was stunning. The fiery orange sun was just beginning to sink below the surface of the water, painting the sky in brilliant shades of lavender, orange, and pink.

A weight settled on her as she watched a handful of surfers out in the frigid water, hoping to catch one last ride before darkness overtook them. Her mind flashed to her best friend, Melissa, insisting on one last ride as the sun set ten years ago. She forced the memory back into its box where it belonged.

Returning to Morro Harbor was the last thing she wanted to do. There was nothing here for her except grief and guilt. She was sure only her grandparents would welcome her. In fact, being back would only stir up memories she was sure most people in

Morro Harbor wanted to keep buried. Her father's sudden death, however, left her little choice but to return. She was his only family, so arrangements fell to her.

Taking one last look at the incoming tide, she pulled out of the parking lot and back onto the highway. Taking the Main Street exit, she drove past Morro Harbor High School. The lights on the football field were just coming on. She almost let herself smile at the memory of the years she'd played soccer there, but she stopped herself. Pushing away the ghosts of the past, she took the next right and headed to Smith Mortuary, the only game in town.

Climbing back into her Jeep ninety minutes later, she leaned her head back and closed her eyes. Making the funeral arrangements had been harder than she'd imagined. She had hoped it would be a simple, emotionless transaction. It was anything but. The funeral home triggered memories of the day she and her father walked through the same door to make the arrangements for her mother. It was eerily quiet, and the sickly floral smell of irises and roses roiled her stomach. She was thankful she hadn't eaten anything since she'd left the Bay Area.

When the single chime over the door sounded, the same reed-thin man in a black suit and tie appeared, just as he had twelve years ago. He had a head full of gray hair now, but the suit and tie looked exactly the same. Just like he had done years ago, Mr. Smith ushered her in to the "coffin room." She quickly explained that her father wanted to be cremated and since she was spreading his ashes in the ocean, she didn't need an expensive urn. The man had looked disappointed but nodded and showed her to the small display in the back corner. She chose the least ostentatious simple black box, signed countless pieces of paper, barely reading them, wrote a check and practically bolted for the door.

The porch light was on when she pulled into the driveway of her maternal grandparents' sky-blue bungalow. Its manicured front lawn was her grandfather's pride and joy. Since he'd retired five years ago from his dental practice, gardening had become Joe Conner's passion.

Pulling her duffel from the back of the Jeep, the sweet fragrance of the gardenias reminded her of her mother. They had been her favorite. Closing the tailgate, she heard a tiny dog's bark and the screech of the screen door. She turned to see Mikey, her grandparents' four-year-old Yorkie racing at her. She suspected the tiny terror had been a German shepherd in a previous life. He feared nothing except a bath. She reached down and picked him up. He welcomed her with doggie kisses all over her face.

"Mikey," she laughed, "I'm happy to see you too." She set him on the ground as her grandmother, Betty Conner, hurried toward her.

"Devin!" The spry, gray-haired woman hugged her while Mikey ran around their feet, barking in excitement.

Devin returned the embrace. Relishing the aroma of warm cookies, she knew her grandmother was baking just for her. "Hi, Grandma." She released the older woman. "The yard looks great."

"It gives your grandfather something to do."

Devin picked up her bag, and they walked to the front door. Just as she reached for the handle, it swung open, and a handsome gray-haired man stepped out and wrapped her in a hug.

"About time you got here. I was about to send out a search party."

Wrapping her arms around her grandfather, she squeezed tightly. "Hi, Grandpa." Letting go, she stepped back, and pointed at Mikey, now in her grandmother's arms. "If you were going to send him, I don't think he'd be much help finding anything other than where the treats are hidden."

Her grandmother lifted the little dog to her face and kissed him on the nose. "Don't you listen to her, Mikey." She put the tiny tornado down and pulled open the screen door. "Come on in. You must be hungry."

The smell of roasted chicken greeted her as she stepped across the threshold.

"Dinner's ready," her grandmother called over her shoulder as they entered the kitchen.

"Your grandfather made an apple pie for dessert. He's become quite the baker."

Beaming, her grandfather's smile spread from ear to ear. He reached down and picked up Devin's duffel. "I'll take this upstairs for you."

"You don't need to do that, Grandpa," Devin protested.

"I may be retired, but I'm in good enough shape to haul your gear upstairs." He smiled. "You stay here and help your grandmother."

Devin turned to her grandmother. "He's just as stubborn as ever, isn't he?"

Her grandmother smiled. "Some things never change," she said as she moved the chicken from the oven onto a platter.

"How did it go at the mortuary?" Devin's grandfather asked as he reentered the kitchen.

She hesitated before answering. "It was like déjà vu." She took a bowl of mashed potatoes to the table. "The place hasn't changed at all since Mom's funeral. Even Mr. Smith looked the same, other than his hair's gone gray." She saw her grandparents looking at each other. They remembered their daughter's funeral all too well.

"As for my father. He wanted to be cremated, and no funeral. So, all I had to do was sign papers and write them a check." Her eyes were dry. She wasn't going to shed a tear for the man who after her mother's death, forgot he had a daughter and lost himself in a bottle of booze.

"He also wanted all his friends to gather at Flybridge Saloon for a round of drinks on him. I'll go by there and set it up for Friday night."

Her grandmother placed the chicken and green beans on the table. "I thought you hadn't spoken to your father since you left."

"I hadn't. Frank called. He said my father told him years ago what he wanted."

"I'm glad you and Frank stayed in contact. He's a good man," her grandfather said.

Devin pulled out a chair. "Even though he was my father's best friend, he's always been there for me." Devin placed her napkin in her lap. "Despite my father."

Her grandmother took a seat and handed Devin the mashed potatoes. "Are you going to stay?"

Devin shook her head. "Only as long as it takes me to clean out and sell the house," she said, not looking up as she spooned potatoes onto her plate.

"You should at least see your friends while you're here," her grandmother said. "Maybe Keri?"

Devin closed her eyes, took a deep breath, then opened them. "I don't plan on being here long enough to reconnect with anyone."

"Will you be going back to Haywood?" her grandfather asked.

Devin shook her head as she poured gravy on her potatoes. "I don't know." She speared a green bean.

Her grandmother looked at her grandfather, her brow furrowed. "What about your apartment?"

Devin didn't look up, suddenly very focused on buttering a roll. "Cleaned it out two weeks ago and handed the keys back to the manager." She picked up her water glass and took a drink. "I've been sleeping on a friend's couch while I finished physical therapy."

"How's that coming along?" her grandmother asked.

"I'm done." A shadow crossed her face. "I doubt my arm will ever be a hundred percent," she replied, not looking up.

"I hope that woman is still in jail," her grandfather mumbled.

Devin set her fork down and looked from her grandfather to her grandmother. "Can we not talk about this right now? I have enough to deal with without thinking about my lying, corrupt ex-girlfriend who almost got me killed." She paused, inhaled and calmly let it out. "I may never be able to go back to work. I'm stuck in limbo until the doctor and psych clear me. If they ever do." She leaned back in her chair, looking from one grandparent to the other. "I don't know if I even want to go back."

Silence hung in the air. Her grandfather stood. "I'll get the pie."

CHAPTER TWO

Devin woke early and just as the sun crested the hills that separated Morro Harbor from the rest of the county, quietly left her grandparents' house. She didn't have the same upper body strength she'd had a year ago, and the strain on her injured arm was painful, but she pushed through and loaded her grandfather's kayak onto the top of the Jeep. She drove to the far end of the harbor, where the locals launched their kayaks and paddleboards. The weather was ideal, with no wind and a slack tide. The water was like glass.

She put on a life jacket and a black Giants baseball cap, dragged the kayak to the water's edge, and climbed in, only getting one foot wet. She pushed off, stuck the paddle in on the starboard side. Pulling back slowly, the kayak glided out into the harbor.

Pulling the paddle through the water on the port side was more difficult. Although healed, her left bicep wasn't as strong as she'd hoped, even after several months of physical therapy. It would take time, the doctors said, months if not a year, to regain full use. She needed to be patient and let her body, and mind, heal.

Easy for them to say. They're not forced to sit around twiddling their thumbs.

Gritting her teeth, she continued to paddle. Even though it was painful, the physical exertion felt good. With every stroke, pent-up tension eased, both mentally and physically. As she fell into a meditative rhythm, she became more aware of her surroundings, the seagull gliding overhead, a pelican, wings tucked in tight, diving into the water to catch a fish, and the ripples it created lapping against her kayak.

The rising sun and gentle breeze helped clear her head. This was what she needed—time to let go of everything and focus on herself. She needed a plan. What would she do if she couldn't be a cop again? She'd never wanted to be anything else. She never had a plan B.

As she paddled, she took notice of the colorful shops and businesses that lined the Embarcadero. A few with back doors gave owners easy access to the marina, where sailboats, fishing trawlers, and a small yacht were docked. Her father's boat was moored near the Coast Guard station at the other end of the harbor. She knew she should check on it but wasn't in a hurry.

On her return to the boat launch she paused to watch a pair of otters frolic in the water. Taking off her cap, her sandy-blond bangs falling over her eyes, she turned her face to the sun, closed her eyes and took in the peacefulness of the morning, and she allowed herself to admit how much she had missed this piece of her past. An hour after setting off she climbed out of the kayak and hauled it back to the parking lot. As she struggled to lift it back on the Jeep, a late-model pickup pulled in behind her. The sun reflected off the windshield, making it impossible to see who was in it. As the driver's side door opened, she readied herself for a confrontation with her past. So much for the peace she'd found on the water.

The driver stepped out, and she breathed a sigh of relief. It was Frank, her godfather, and her father's best friend. He had been the one who called, explaining that he and her father had been fishing several miles offshore when her father had had a heart attack. Frank had radioed the Coast Guard but by the time they arrived her father was dead.

"You're back," he said, his arms outstretched.

She walked into his embrace, wrapping her arms around his waist. The reality of her father's death finally hit her. Even though she hadn't spoken to her father in a decade, the emotions she'd kept locked away spilled out, and she sobbed against Frank's shoulder.

He let her cry herself out, rubbing her back, not saying a word. When the tears stopped, he handed her his handkerchief. "How about I help you load that kayak?" he said.

Devin blew her nose and nodded. "Thanks, that would be great."

After securing the kayak, Frank leaned against the Jeep and crossed his arms. "How are you holding up?"

She tried to smile. "It's been a tough year. And now this." She wiped her face on the sleeve of her shirt. "It's a lot." She hid her feelings from most people, even her grandparents. She didn't want them to worry about her. But Frank was different. After her mother died, her father had turned his back on her, but Frank had been there for her. She'd heard her father and Frank arguing about it more than once. Frank had called him a horse's ass, and her father had told him to mind his own business.

Frank nodded. "It is." He headed back to his truck, pausing. "How about we meet at the boat around four o'clock and have a beer?"

She picked up the kayak paddle and tossed it in the back of the Jeep. She wasn't sure how she felt about setting foot on her father's boat. But it was something she was going to have to deal with sooner or later. "Sure. We need to talk about his ashes anyway."

"All right, I'll see you then," he said, driving off with a wave.

Devin climbed into the Jeep and started the engine. She wasn't looking forward to what she had to do next.

After returning the kayak to her grandparents' garage and retrieving her duffel, she drove to her father's one-story house a block from the beach. She pulled into the driveway next to her father's beat-up Chevy Silverado pickup, the blue paint faded by the sun and briny sea air. She sat there, taking in the house where she'd grown up. It hadn't aged well. It had been an ocean-green color, but it had faded to a dull gray and was peeling in several places. There was a spider crack in one of the front windows, and the roof needed attention. A single dandelion in the front yard was the only speck of green. After a decade of drought, she couldn't really blame her father for that. Many of the neighbors had let their yards die out, but most of them replaced them with dry scape that flourished in the moisture the foggy coastal mornings provided.

Pushing aside memories, she gave herself a pep talk and climbed out. As a kid she'd excitedly run up the path to the front door a thousand times. This time her feet dragged with the dread of what she faced inside.

She pulled the key to the house out of her pocket. For years, it had lain untouched, pushed to the back of a drawer in her nightstand. She didn't know why she'd kept it. She hadn't set foot inside the house in over ten years. Probably for this very reason, she mused.

It took effort to get the key to turn in the lock. When it finally did, she pushed the door open, paused and took a breath. Crossing the threshold, she was immediately hit with a barrage of memories, happy and painful. Christmas, birthdays, running through the house laughing with Melissa, bringing home A's on her report card, her mother's diagnosis and the gathering after the funeral. And kissing Keri in her bedroom.

She recalled the hateful words she and her father had exchanged the summer after her high school graduation. After her emotional encounter with Frank, her feelings were raw and close to the surface. She forced down a sob, raised her chin, and steeled herself for what lay ahead.

I can do this.

Walking further into the living room, the mustiness hit her. She wondered if her father ever opened the windows. She made her way around the room, opening them all, allowing sunlight and fresh air in. She walked through the house, avoiding for now, the room that had been hers for eighteen years, letting the morning breeze chase out any ghosts that had taken up residence.

Deciding to start in the kitchen, she opened the refrigerator. Most of the contents had expired weeks before her father had. Only a six-pack of Budweiser, a tub of butter, and a brick of Irish cheese were still good. She poured a carton of milk down the sink, placed everything else on the counter and found a box of garbage bags under the sink. She opened the freezer. Inside were a handful of frost-covered frozen dinners and a years-old pint of jamoca almond fudge ice cream. That was strange. It was her favorite. Her father preferred vanilla. Why would he have a pint of her favorite ice cream? She tossed it into the bag with the other expired food.

She tossed any expired dry goods and cans from the cabinets, setting aside anything still in date to take to her grandparents. She kept a box of mac and cheese, a can of chili with beans, and an unopened box of Ritz crackers.

She carried the sack outside, dropped it in the trash and rolled the can to the curb. As she turned to go back to the house, a voice called out from the house next door.

"Devin, is that you?" An elderly woman in a pink house dress stood on the porch, leaning on a cane.

"Yes, Mrs. Booker, it's me." The Bookers had lived next door to her parents since before Devin was born. She must be in her nineties now, Devin thought.

"I'm so sorry about your father. He was a good man. He always rolled my trash cans out for me."

Devin smiled. "How about I do it for you today?"

"I'd appreciate that. It's just too much for me. You know I'm ninety-two now."

"No way. You don't look a day over eighty," Devin said, chuckling. She walked between the houses and came back, pushing Mrs. Booker's trash can. "There you go, Mrs. Booker," she said, leaving the can at the curb. "Can your son bring it in for you?"

Mrs. Booker shook her head. "No, dear. Bob moved to Oregon last year after he retired."

"What about your grandkids?" She remembered the woman had four grandkids, two older and two younger than Devin.

"No, they've all moved away too."

Devin's heart ached for the old woman. "Okay, I'll get it this week."

"Will you be moving back here, dear?"

Devin shook her head. "No. I'm only here long enough to take care of my father's things."

"Oh." She paused, then asked, "Where are you living now?"

That's a good question. Where do I live? She wasn't sure she wanted to return to Haywood, or anywhere in the Bay Area for that matter. Even if she could return to work, did she want to? Did she want to be a cop somewhere else? Did she want to be a cop at all?

"I was in the Bay Area until recently," she said. "I'm thinking about relocating though."

The remnants of Mrs. Booker's eyebrows scrunched together. "Why not here?"

"What?"

"Why not relocate here? Your father left you the house, didn't he? And I'm sure Joe and Betty would be thrilled to have you nearby."

They're probably the only ones who would be. "I'll give it some thought," she said, knowing full well that moving back to Morro Harbor was never going to happen. "You have a good day, Mrs. Booker."

"You too, dear." Mrs. Booker let the screen door slam behind her.

Devin paused to watch a seagull circle overhead. She closed her eyes and listened to the familiar sound of the ocean, letting the tension in her shoulders ease. She couldn't think of a better place to grow up. It had been perfect, idyllic, until it wasn't.

As she carried another box of odds and ends to the garage, her stomach growled. She glanced at the clock on the stove and was surprised to see it was almost one. No wonder her stomach made itself known. She grabbed her keys and headed to the Jeep. She wondered if the fish taco place on Main Street was still there. A couple of halibut and guacamole tacos sounded good.

Downtown wasn't busy, and traffic was light. As she rounded the corner onto Main Street, she was happy to see the sign for Manny's Tacos on the next block. Pulling into an empty space, she shut off the engine. Other than a recent coat of paint, the stand-alone building hadn't changed much. The large sign, a taco shell with a cartoon fish, and a Taco Tuesday poster still hung on the building. However, the Tuesday special was now three tacos for ten dollars, instead of three for three. Nothing stays the same, she thought.

Her mind flashed to the hundreds of times she, Melissa, Keri, and Bo had come here for a quick bite after school or to hang out after a day of surfing. For a second, she thought she heard Melissa's laugh. She swallowed down a sob that threatened to explode from deep inside.

Sucking in a large gulp of air, she blinked away the tears, and walked to the door, her head up and her shoulders pulled back. The bell over the door tinkled, and several faces looked up. She let out a sigh and relaxed a little. She didn't recognize anybody. The last thing she wanted was an unpleasant interaction with the past.

She placed her order and settled into a booth away from the other patrons. She pulled out her phone and brought up her email account. The first three were garbage, and she hit delete without opening them. The fourth, however, caused her jaw to clench. It was from Tracy. She stared at the three words in the subject line:

I MISS YOU.

The audacity of it made her blood boil. The woman had nearly gotten her killed. Not to mention lied to her and made her look like a fool. And now she had the nerve to say she missed her. Unbelievable. She knew she should just delete it without reading it, but...

Devin,

I haven't seen or heard from you in almost three months. Why won't you answer my calls? I'm worried sick. I know you blame me for everything that happened, but honestly, it wasn't all my fault. You have to take some responsibility. You didn't have to go to Internal Affairs. We could have figured out a way to fix things. I thought you loved me.

Because of this mess, no police department will hire me. I can't even get work as a security guard. I don't know what to do. Since you kicked me out, I've been staying with my sister, but she told me today I need to find my own place by the end of the month. Devin, I need you. Can't you forgive me and come back? Please, Devin, I miss you. Please call me.

I Love You,
Tracy

She slammed the phone on the table. Several heads turned to look her way.

Un-fucking-believable.

Tracy had abused her authority as a police officer right under Devin's nose. She'd lied to everyone. She'd even lied under oath. She'd stolen cash and jewelry, albeit from criminals, but it was still wrong. She'd extorted money from a local pub and cardroom owner. And until six months ago, Devin hadn't had a clue. They were living under the same roof, sleeping in the same bed, and Devin hadn't suspected a thing. That was until Tracy came home with a brand new Platinum Edition Porsche Cayenne. There was no way she could afford it on a cop's salary. And as far as Devin knew, Tracy hadn't inherited money from a rich uncle. She claimed she'd been saving for it. But there was no way in hell she could have saved enough for a big enough down payment in the six years she'd been a cop to make the payments manageable.

That was when Devin went to Internal Affairs. The IA investigation discovered another three officers were involved. Tracy struck a deal to roll over on the others in exchange for not being prosecuted. But they did fire her.

Doing the right thing had almost cost Devin her life. Crossing the thin blue line was a betrayal. Being a cop meant you were part of a brotherhood that demanded unconditional loyalty. So, when the other cops learned Tracy had been fired and three officers arrested, they turned their backs on Devin. She was persona non grata. Not only did they give her the cold shoulder, they failed to assist when she radioed for backup. She'd responded to a burglary in progress. When she arrived at the scene, shots rang out. She radioed for backup, dispatch sent out the call to all units, but no one responded. There was only silence. No one came to her aid.

She'd been shot in the upper arm. The bullet continued into her rib cage, then her lung. If it hadn't been for a Good Samaritan calling 911 and stanching the blood until an ambulance and paramedics arrived, she probably would have bled to death. Unsurprisingly, the crime remained unsolved.

She'd undergone a six-hour surgery to repair her arm and remove the bullet from her lung. It took eight weeks for her to heal, then three months of physical therapy. Her arm was still weak, and she still couldn't take a full breath. She might never be one hundred percent. She remained in limbo, unable to work, but because she was injured in the line of duty, she was still drawing a paycheck.

"Devin," a voice rang out. "Your order's ready."

After lunch, she strolled past the quaint shops along the harbor. Bright hues covered the old brick and clapboard buildings, some adorned with window boxes full of flowers. The smell of salt and sea filled her nostrils as seagulls squawked overhead. She'd forgotten how beautiful the town was.

As she continued down the street, she passed several old buildings that brought back childhood memories. A few businesses that had been there years ago were gone, but many were still there. In between the bookstore she had frequented with her mother and the Wine Time wine bar was an empty storefront. It was prime space. She wondered what had occupied it.

Stopping in front of the bookstore, she smiled at the rainbow flag that hung out front. The sign on the window said Rainbow Books. She walked in. The bell overhead tinkled merrily, and she smiled to herself as fond memories came rushing back. Even though the name had changed, it was just like she remembered. The bookshelves were interspersed with comfortable chairs for visitors to relax and escape into another world.

She located a copy of her favorite childhood book, *James and the Giant Peach*. Her mother had read it to her countless times. Everything about this place brought back memories.

"Devin Davis?"

Although the voice behind her didn't sound angry or unwelcoming, her shoulders tensed. She returned the book to the shelf and slowly turned around. The face was older, but the smile was the same. "Chris!"

Chris Curtis had lived down the street from her their whole lives. They'd gone to preschool together and remained friends throughout school until she'd left town without so much as a goodbye.

The slightly built man squealed like a child and ran over so fast to wrap his arms around her neck that she nearly fell over. She returned the hug with one arm and grabbed onto the bookcase with the other, keeping them both upright. Chris pulled back slightly but didn't let go. "I wondered when you'd show up." His smile stretched from ear to ear. "It's so good to see you."

Devin smiled back, the tension of the moment slipping away.

He let her go and took a step back. "I'm sorry about your father."

Devin sighed and nodded. "I hadn't talked to him since I left."

"Chris, where'd you go?" a deep male voice called out from the back of the store.

Chris smiled. "That's my husband. I'm supposed to be getting a broom. Come on I'll introduce you." He motioned for Devin to follow him. "I'm coming, sweetheart," he called out.

He led her through the maze of bookcases to the back of the store. A tall, muscular man with a neatly trimmed ginger beard stood with his hands on his hips. "What took you so long?"

Chris introduced Devin to his husband with as much aplomb as Vanna White revealing the correct letters on Wheel of Fortune. "Devin, may I present my husband, Billy Ferguson. Husband, this is one of my oldest and dearest friends, Devin Davis."

"Most people call me Bill," he said, holding out his hand.

Devin took the offered hand and shook it. "It's a pleasure to meet you, Bill."

"Chris, did you get the broom?" Bill asked.

"Oops. I'll be right back," he said as he hurried off.

Bill shook his head. "I love him to death, but sometimes he's a complete airhead."

Devin laughed. "I guess some things never change."

Before Devin could say anything else, Chris returned. "Found it!" he said, handing the broom over to his husband.

"Thanks, babe." Bill began sweeping the floor.

Chris grabbed Devin's hand. "Billy, we'll be upfront. My girl and I have a lot of catching up to do."

"Okay, babe, don't forget Ms. Bell is stopping by this afternoon."

"Ms. Bell, our English teacher?" Devin asked.

Chris nodded but kept walking back to the front of the shop. "That's the one." He motioned for Devin to have a seat on the stool across from the cashier counter.

"She was always supportive. Especially after Melissa died."

"She hasn't changed. She's still as sweet as can be," Chris said as he straightened a stack of books on the counter.

"So, who owns the bookstore now?"

Chris let out a laugh. "We do. We bought it from Mr. Walters a few years ago. He wanted to sell, and Billy couldn't imagine Morro Harbor without a bookstore and insisted we buy it. The rest is history."

"I thought you wanted to be a nurse."

"I am. I got my nursing certificate. I work part-time at an independent living facility in San Luis Obispo. Billy has a degree in business. He's the one with experience. He was the manager at Barnes and Noble when I met him." Chris smiled. "But enough about me. How long are you here? We're hosting a book signing for Ms. Bell on Saturday."

"Ms. Bell wrote a book?"

"She did. It's a collection of her poems."

"Well good for her. I'll have to pick up a copy."

Chris winked. "I think I can set you up." He grinned. "So, will you come Saturday? Keri will be here."

Devin frowned. "I'm surprised she stayed."

Chris shook his head. "She went to Cal Poly. She owns the wine bar a couple of doors down the street. It opens at two, you should stop in and see her."

"I can't, and I'm sure she wouldn't want to see me." She stood. "On Friday my dad's buying a round of drinks at Flybridge. You and Bill should come."

"Okay, if you'll come to the book signing Saturday."

Devin sighed. "I'm trying to keep a low profile while I'm here."

"That's ridiculous. This is your hometown."

"That doesn't mean I'm welcome here. Some things people never forget. Or forgive."

Chris placed a hand on her arm. "Devin, it wasn't your fault. No one blames you. Not then, not now."

Devin looked out the window, blinking several times to fend off tears. She smiled when she saw Ms. Bell standing outside. "Chris, I'm going to go say hi to Ms. Bell. I'll see you Friday?"

Chris nodded. "We'll be there."

Devin smiled, then stepped out of the shop. "Ms. Bell?" she said, unsure of what reaction she'd receive.

The petite older woman stopped and turned around. "Devin, is that you?" The woman's face lit up as she reached out to hug her ex-pupil.

Devin stooped to return the hug. "Yes, Ms. Bell, it's me."

She let go of Devin. "You're not a student. I think you can call me Liz now."

Devin grinned. "I don't know. I think you'll always be Ms. Bell to me."

Liz shook her head. "I was so sorry to hear of your father's passing. Will there be a service?"

Devin frowned. "No. He didn't want one. He'll be cremated. Frank and I will take his ashes out on the boat."

The older woman nodded. "Appropriate for a lifelong fisherman, I suppose."

Devin shrugged. "I guess."

"Are you back for good?"

"No, only as long as it takes to handle my dad's affairs and sell the—"

Both women jumped at the squeal of tires screeching to a stop next to them. The driver's side door of a full-size black truck flew open. A young man in his late twenties, with unkept black hair and a face that hadn't seen a shave in several days shot out and pointed at Devin.

"What the hell are you doing here?" Bo Bailey, Melissa's twin brother, demanded. His face glowed crimson. He did not look anything like the boy with whom she had grown up, surfed and had bonfires on the beach.

"Bo, stop it. She has every right to be here," Liz scolded him.

He glared at the older woman then refocused his anger on Devin. "You know you're not welcome here."

Devin ground her teeth, determined not to cry in front of him.

"That's enough, Bo." Liz raised her voice. "That's enough."

People on the street had stopped to watch the commotion. Chris and Bill walked out of the shop.

"Bo, you should leave. The police are on their way. You don't need another run in with them," Bill warned.

"Fuck you, Bill," Bo spat, then glared at Devin. "Watch your back."

Devin's jaw dropped. "What's that supposed to mean?"

"Leave," he said. He glared one last time at Ms. Bell before turning abruptly and climbing back into the truck. He gunned the engine and raced away, tires squealing, leaving a fog of burnt rubber in the air.

Just as Chris and Bill stepped up next to Devin and Ms. Bell, a black-and-white SUV pulled to the curb in front of the bookstore. A tall attractive dark-haired woman in a police uniform stepped out. Devin guessed she was in her late thirties.

"Good morning," she said to the four of them.

"Miranda. I didn't expect you to show up," Chris said.

The woman smiled at Chris. "I was only a block away."

Chris motioned to Devin. "Devin, this is Chief Miranda Taylor. Chief, this is Devin Davis, she's a friend from high school."

Devin held out her hand. "Nice to meet you."

The officer's eyes narrowed, hesitating for a moment before taking Devin's hand.

"Ms. Davis."

"Devin's a cop up in the Bay Area," Chris said.

"Is that so?"

"Actually, I'm on leave. I was injured."

Chris looked at her, his eyebrows scrunched together. "Really?"

Devin shrugged. "It's not a big deal."

The chief turned away from Devin and looked at Liz. "So, what happened here?"

Devin retreated a step, wondering why the woman was as cold as an ice cube. Did she know about Melissa's death and Devin's role in it? She couldn't think of any other reason for the woman to be so icy.

"We were standing here talking. Bo screeched to a stop, got out and started yelling at us."

The chief faced Devin. "Why?"

Feeling like she was being interrogated, Devin hesitated before answering. After counting to five she said, "He's hated me ever since his sister died. He blames me."

The chief crossed her arms and continued to glare at Devin. "Why? What did you do?"

Chris took a step forward. "What the hell, Miranda? Why the third degree?"

She stared at him. "That's Chief Taylor to you."

"Seriously? What's happening here? Oh, I know." He shook his head. "Keri told you about Devin and you're worried they'll hook up."

Both women stared at him. "What?" they said in unison.

"Are you crazy?" Devin asked. "I haven't seen Keri in over ten years."

Chris raised an eyebrow. "So?"

"So, we were just kids. And it was a long time ago."

"So?" He smiled. "You're back now."

Miranda cleared her throat. "I don't care what may or may not be going on between the two of them…"

"There's nothing going on. I haven't even seen her."

Miranda, a few inches taller than Devin's five foot eight, scowled down at her.

Chris held out his hands. "Okay, you two. Back to your corners."

Miranda took a step toward her vehicle, then turned back to Chris. "I'll have my guys pull Bo over and give him a warning." She glared at Devin one last time, continued to her car, and drove away. Neither Devin nor Chris said a word until the car turned the corner and was out of sight.

"What the hell is wrong with her?" Devin asked.

Chris shook his head. "She didn't take the breakup well."

"What breakup?"

"She and Keri were a thing. Keri broke it off. Miranda didn't take it well."

"Why'd they break up?"

Chris shrugged. "You'd have to ask Keri." He paused. "But I'm guessing Miranda knows about you and Keri."

Devin shook her head. "There is no me and Keri."

Chris smiled. "But there was in high school."

Devin stared at him.

"Well, I can't think of another reason she'd treat you like that. I mean, aren't cops like some kind of fraternity?"

"Some would say it's a legalized gang."

"Hmm. Sounds like there's more to that story."

"There is, but let's save it for another time. I need to get going." She looked at Liz. "My father's buying a round of drinks at Flybridge Friday night. You should come."

"How nice of you to buy a round for your dad's friends," Ms. Bell said.

"It's on his credit card, not mine." She turned to Chris and Bill. "You'll come, right? You can keep me company."

Bill put his arm across Chris's shoulders. "Sure, we'll be there."

She looked at Ms. Bell. "You too?"

"I'd love to."

"Great, I'll see you all then," Devin said and strode off down the street.

CHAPTER THREE

Carrying a small red ice chest, Devin climbed aboard her father's boat. She set the chest down, stretched her neck from side to side, then bent over and touched her fingertips to her toes. Her glutes and hamstrings screamed in protest, but she held on for a full minute. The hour she'd spent kayaking that morning had stressed muscles she hadn't used in far too long. As she took out a beer, she heard footsteps behind her. She turned around and smiled.

"Hi, Frank."

He stepped onto the boat. There was a slack tide, so the water was calm, making it easy to climb aboard.

"Hey, Devin," he said with a nod. He wrapped his arms around her. "How ya doing?"

"I'm okay," she said noncommittally as she screwed the top off the beer and took a sip.

"There's beer in the ice chest. Help yourself."

"Thanks," he said, taking a beer.

"It feels strange being on the boat without him," Devin said, her voice flat. "I keep thinking he's going to come up from below and yell at me. Or ignore me." She looked out across the harbor and wiped away a tear. "He never, in all that time, reached out to me. Not once."

Frank put his arm around her shoulder. "Your dad was a stubborn man," he said. "He let his pride get in the way."

Devin nodded and wiped her eyes. "I know," she said. "But I wish he had. Even if it was just to let me know he was alive." She rubbed her face with both hands. "Enough of that. How have you been?"

For the next half hour, they sat on the boat, laughing and reminiscing. Remembering the good times before her mother died and her father became a drunk.

"His ashes will be ready Friday afternoon," Devin said, finishing her beer and tossing the bottle into the ice chest. "Does Saturday at sunrise work for you? I'd like to get this behind me."

Frank nodded in agreement. "Saturday at sunrise sounds good."

Neither one spoke for a few minutes, lost in their own thoughts, enjoying the quiet of the harbor, the water lapping against the side of the boat, and the squadron of pelicans overhead.

Frank stood and returned his empty bottle to the ice chest. "He did love you."

Devin sighed and looked at him. "He had a strange way of showing it."

Frank nodded. "Let me know if you need anything. I'll see you bright and early Saturday." He stepped over the side of the boat onto the dock.

"Oh, Frank, can you let Dad's friends know he's buying a round of drinks at Flybridge Friday night?"

"Sure thing. I'll see ya then."

"Thanks, Frank."

Devin turned back to the water. A pair of otters floated by in the slow-moving current, their bodies bobbing in the wake of a passing boat. One rolled onto its back, grooming its whiskers, while the other dove beneath the surface with a quick flick of its tail. She opened another beer and let the weight of everything fade away.

CHAPTER FOUR

Devin dropped the empty boxes she'd picked up in town in front of the door to her old room. She hadn't entered it yet and didn't know what she'd face on the other side. Had her father, not wanting to have any reminders of his deviant daughter, gotten rid of her things? Or would everything, including the ghosts, be inside waiting for her?

She pushed open the door to have the past hit her in the face. Everything was exactly as she'd left it ten years ago. Her soccer cleats, caked with mud, were still on the floor where she'd kicked them off the day before she left. The day her father had walked in without knocking and caught her and Keri making out, Devin's hand under Keri's shirt. They'd jumped apart.

"Dad," she'd said, her eyes wide.

He glared at Keri. "Get out!"

Keri turned to Devin, a mix of confusion and fear on her face.

Devin nodded. "I'll call you later."

Keri had hurried past Devin's father without looking at him.

Devin forced herself to remain calm in the face of her father's anger. He stood there, his fists clenched at his sides, his face glowing red. "What the hell was that, Devin?"

She could smell alcohol on his breath. That wasn't a surprise. "I'm gay," she said, her voice unwavering.

"The hell you are," he yelled. "Not in my house you aren't."

"Dad, I'm not going to pretend I'm not."

"I won't have a queer under my roof."

Devin recoiled, her mind reeling from the unexpected venom of her father's words. In her eighteen years, even at his drunkest, she'd never seen this side of him.

"Dad—"

"Get out of my house." He pointed at the door.

Devin felt like she'd been punched in the gut. She opened her mouth, but her brain couldn't find the words.

"I mean it. Get out."

Without a second thought, Devin grabbed her sweatshirt, Converse high-tops, and car keys. "I'll be back tomorrow while you're out to pack my things."

She rushed past him and hurried out the front door. She'd spent the night at her grandparents, telling them she'd had an argument with her father, but not going into detail. The next morning, she returned to the house, no longer her home, packed up her things, and left for college early. Her grandparents tried to talk her into staying with them, but her mind was made up. She was leaving and vowed never to set foot in Morro Harbor as long as her father was alive.

Her only regret was the hastily written note she'd left Keri. She'd been a coward, afraid to say goodbye in person, knowing Keri was the only one who could talk her out of leaving.

Now her father was dead, and she had no choice but to return and deal with the remains of his life as quickly as she could. Hopefully without opening the old wounds she'd locked away.

Picking up an empty box, she walked to the dresser, now covered in a thick layer of dust, and picked up a photo of her and Melissa with their surfboards, smiles so wide it was almost painful to see. Keri had taken the picture a week before Melissa drowned. She set the picture aside and began filling the box with knickknacks from her childhood. She opened drawers, pulling out T-shirts and shorts long out of style. There was a blue hoodie with the high school logo. She pulled it on. It still fit and she decided to keep it.

She rummaged through the rest of the drawers, pulling out a half dozen swimsuits, and unceremoniously dropped them in the box of things to get rid of. She hadn't stepped foot in the ocean since Melissa's death.

Opening another drawer, she stumbled upon a picture album filled with hers and Melissa's surfing adventures. She let out a sob and sank to the floor. For the first time in years, she let herself grieve for her best friend. When she couldn't cry anymore, she wiped her face with the sleeve of the hoodie and closed the album, adding it to a separate box of things she wanted to keep.

Turning to the bright-pink surfboard that hung on the wall over the twin bed, she thought back to the day she and Melissa had bought them. They were thirteen. She'd convinced Melissa they should get matching surfboards and learn to surf. They'd saved up their allowances and money from odd jobs and babysitting. She wondered what in the world they had been thinking, getting Day-Glo pink surfboards. But they loved them, and they certainly stood out on the waves. When they started high school two years later, they joined the surf team and replaced the pink boards with more traditional ones. But they'd kept them as reminders of their friendship.

She pulled the board off the wall and carried it to the garage. She couldn't bear to keep it but couldn't bring herself to get rid of it either. Maybe she'd donate it to the surf school.

Walking back to the bedroom, she wondered what Melissa's family had done with the matching board, then wondered about Melissa's parents and younger sister, Wren. Did they still blame her? She'd learned firsthand that Bo sure did.

As she worked, she found old photos and mementos from their childhood adventures—scrapbooks filled with pictures of them at the beach, camping trips, and other memories that made her smile. In one corner was a note Melissa had written to her in the sixth grade. She hadn't seen it since, but she remembered the contents even now. In loopy cursive writing it said, "You're my best friend always and I love you no matter what."

Devin folded the note and slipped it into the box with the picture of the two of them. She took down more photos and put them in the to-get-rid-of box—surfing and soccer trophies, shells, sand dollars, CDs, flip-flops, and soccer cleats. There were so many wonderful memories. But the overwhelming sadness knowing that she was to blame for Melissa's death overshadowed everything. Not even the scholarship she'd set up at the high school for the girls' surf team lessened her guilt.

Exhausted, she taped another box shut. The room had grown dark, and she turned on the lights as she carried a box to the garage. In the kitchen she opened the refrigerator. Her father's beer and cheese and crackers weren't enough for dinner. Not wanting to face anyone, she opened the Instacart App on her phone and placed an order. She fell onto the couch and turned on the TV while she waited.

Pounding on the door woke Devin with a start. The local weather person in a blue suit and pink tie was waving a hand around on a map, saying something about the offshore winds. The pounding continued and her muscles screamed in protest as she stood.

She turned the doorknob as the pounding started again. "Okay—" She froze. Her heart pounded in her ears, and her breathing quickened. It wasn't possible. She was dead. Melissa couldn't be standing in front of her, holding two large grocery bags, looking very much alive.

"Relax, Devin," the young woman said. "Can I come in?"

Devin nodded and took a step back. The young woman, with Melissa's jet-black hair, walked past her, set the bags on the coffee table and turned to face her, hands in the pockets of her sweatshirt. The young woman smiled. "I'm not a ghost, Devin."

"Wren?" Bo and Melissa's little sister? She was only nine or ten when Melissa died. This person was at least eighteen or nineteen and as tall as Devin.

The young woman nodded. "Yes," she said, taking the two steps that separated them and wrapping her arms around Devin's neck.

Devin just stood there, unsure what to think or feel. Then she wrapped her arms around her best friend's little sister and squeezed her tight. Finally, she pulled herself together and motioned to the couch. "Can you stay for a while?"

Wren nodded. "I was leaving work when I saw your name on the delivery, so I grabbed it." She sat near the middle of the couch. "I'm sorry about your father. It was a shock to the whole town."

Devin schooled her features and nodded. "I hadn't talked to him in a decade."

Wren cocked her head to the side. "Why not?"

Devin sighed. "We had a huge argument, and he gave me an ultimatum. I chose to leave rather than pretend to be something I wasn't."

Wren leaned her head to the side. "He found out you're gay?"

"How did you know? You were just a little kid when I left."

Wren smiled. "I was pretty astute for a kid. And I overheard you and Melissa talking a few months before she died."

"I told her I was gay."

Wren nodded. "And that you liked Keri."

Devin smiled. "That was what the argument with my dad was about. He walked in and caught us making out. He went ballistic. It was pretty ugly."

"I'm so sorry." She placed her hand on top of Devin's. "He never reached out? Never apologized?"

Devin shook her head. "No. And neither did I."

"Do your grandparents know what happened?"

Devin nodded.

"And you left and never came back."

Devin pressed her lips together and nodded.

Neither of them said anything, just sat with the ghosts in the room, until Wren asked, "Can you tell me about the accident?"

Devin hung her head.

Wren continued, "All I know is she drowned while surfing with you. My parents still won't talk about it. Bo thinks it was your fault. That you're to blame. I don't know what to believe." She leaned forward, elbows on knees, and waited for Devin to respond.

Devin could feel her heart pounding. Even though it was difficult, Wren deserved to know the truth. She took a moment to collect herself then recounted the events of the worst day of her life.

"We went to Dunes Beach to surf, just like we'd done a thousand times. Bo dropped us off. He was going to surf with us, but his girlfriend called and said her parents were out of town, so he rushed over to her house." She looked at the floor, remembering. "The waves were perfect. The weather was perfect." Devin closed her eyes, remembering the cloudless autumn day. The wind was minimal, the waves came in perfect sets. They couldn't have asked for better conditions.

"A little after seven, the sun was nearly gone. I yelled to Melissa that we could get one more ride in before it got too dark." She looked up at the ceiling, tears pooling in her eyes. "We both caught a wave that walled up and we rode it all the way in. It was a perfect way to end the day." Devin looked at Wren. "But Melissa wanted one more. I told her it was too dark, but she wouldn't listen and paddled back out." Devin paused and wiped away tears with the back of her hand. "Within a minute of paddling out, she caught an eight-footer and rode it until it swallowed her. The leash on her ankle broke, the board flew straight up and hit her when it came down. I knew she was in trouble. I started running and yelling for someone to call 911. I dove in and swam out to her. The current kept pulling me back and it took forever to get to her. She was face down in the water. I turned her over and pulled her back to shore. I started CPR as soon as I had her out of the water."

Wren, her face wet with tears, scooted over and put her arm around Devin's shoulders.

Devin continued, "I don't know how long it took for the rescue squad to get there but it seemed like hours. I never stopped pumping her chest. Paramedics pulled me off and they loaded her onto a stretcher and rushed her into an ambulance." Her voice shook. "They wouldn't let me go with her. I didn't have a ride, so I sat in the sand and cried. At some point, Keri showed up. Someone must have called her. She drove me to the hospital.

"When I walked in, your dad was holding your mom. She was hysterical. Then Bo charged at me, yelling that it was my fault." She let out a sob. "That it was my fault Melissa was dead. I don't remember anything else about that day. I don't remember much else until the funeral."

They sat in silence for a few moments until Wren spoke up. "It wasn't your fault, Devin. It was nobody's fault. Melissa made a poor choice, and it cost her her life."

Devin looked out the window. Even if that were true it didn't stop her from feeling guilty. "Bo still thinks it's my fault. As I was leaving the bookstore this afternoon, he stopped his truck in the middle of the street and started yelling at me and Ms. Bell. I guess he still blames her for failing him and losing his scholarship."

"Bo hasn't been the same since she died. He drinks way too much. He's barely hanging on to his job." She blew out her breath. "We don't know what to do. He's so angry. He lashes out at everyone. But he's wrong to blame you. You couldn't have prevented Melissa from staying out in the water. And I'm sure Ms. Bell did everything she could to help Bo pass that class. But he was angry and grieving and didn't care about anything." She placed her hand on Devin's. "You can't let him guilt-trip you into thinking otherwise."

Devin nodded. A tiny part of her knew Wren was right. It wasn't her fault, but that didn't make the pain any less real. "Thanks," she whispered, grateful for her comfort and understanding. The two of them sat in silence for a few more moments, each lost in their own thoughts and grief.

"Do you still surf?"

Devin shook her head. "I haven't been on a board since that day."

"Neither has Bo." Wren gave her a sad smile. "I never learned how. My parents forbade it. They were too afraid something would happen to me."

Devin pursed her lips before saying anything. "You can't blame them, can you?"

"No, I guess not. But I'm an adult now. It's not up to them."
She paused. "I want to find out why my sister loved it so much."

Devin clasped her hands, her knuckles turning white. "I can't
help you, Wren. I can't go back out there."

"I understand," she said, disappointment clear in her voice. "I
still have homework to finish, so I should get going."

Devin walked her to the door. Wren paused, then turned and
hugged Devin. "I hope we can spend some time together while
you're here."

Devin nodded and blinked back tears.

Wren gave a little wave as she walked down the path and
drove away.

Devin took one of her father's beers from the refrigerator.
Exhaustion from the emotions she'd shoved down for so long
engulfed her. She opened the can, drank down half and grimaced
at the taste.

CHAPTER FIVE

What the hell just happened? What was that explosion? What the hell hit me so hard it slammed me to the ground? Shit, where did my gun go? My arm and chest feel like someone took a branding iron to them. The pain feels like molten lava running through my veins. It hurts so much I can't breathe. I can't scream. I'm on the floor, staring at the ceiling of a warehouse, trying to breathe, trying to stay awake. Keri's here. How did she get here? Why is she here? She lifts my head and rests it in her lap. She runs her hand through my hair. She's crying. Am I dying? I try to reach up and touch her face, but I can't lift my arm. I open my mouth to tell her not to cry, but nothing comes out.

There's a phone ringing in the distance. I wish someone would answer it. I can't get up, and I don't want Keri to leave me. Someone answer the damn phone!

Keri keeps looking into my face and touching my cheek with her hand. There are tears in her eyes.

The ringing won't stop. It fills the room and reverberates off the walls. Answer the goddamn phone!

Devin bolted upright, not sure where she was. Her heart raced and perspiration dotted her forehead. Her phone rang, and she stared at it, taking a second to get her bearings. The sun was up. She was in her father's house, not the dark warehouse where she'd been shot. It had been a dream. No, a nightmare. Keri hadn't been in the warehouse the night of the shooting. Why was Keri in her nightmare? She hadn't had any contact with her since she'd walked away from her and Morro Harbor.

Reluctantly, she reached for her phone. She didn't recognize the number. She braced herself for whoever it might be and pushed the button. "Hello?"

"Is this Devin Davis?" The voice was all business.

"Yes," she answered.

"Good morning. This is Gerald Williams. Please accept my condolences."

Devin ran her hand through her tangled hair. "Thank you."

The man continued, "I played golf with your grandfather yesterday and he mentioned you were in town. He wasn't sure if you knew I had prepared your father's trust, and suggested I reach out to you about it." He paused. "Would it be possible for you to come to my office this afternoon so we can go over it?"

Devin leaned forward on the couch and rubbed her forehead. "What time?"

"Does two o'clock work for you?"

"Sure. I'll be there."

She looked at the clock—nine a.m.—then at the five empty beer cans on the coffee table. That explained the pounding in her head, and queasy stomach. As she slowly stood, the dream still clung to her memory. Why was Keri in it? She gathered the beer cans, headed for the kitchen and tossed them in the trash. Turning to the coffee maker, she dropped a filter in and scooped grounds into the basket, poured water in and pushed the green button.

While she waited for the coffee to brew, she gazed out of the window. Fog hung heavily in the morning marine air. It drifted like a ghost across the backyard, obscuring everything in its cloudy embrace. The sound of the town's mournful foghorn echoed in the distance. Her thoughts turned to Keri and the letter she'd left ending their relationship.

Keri,

My Dad threw me out.

I'm leaving town.

I'm sorry,

Devin

Keri had written and called and texted, but Devin hadn't answered any of them. She regretted it now. The way she left, without a real explanation or goodbye, was cowardly.

Devin poured coffee into a stained mug she'd given to her dad for Father's Day many years ago. Her mind flashed back to the dream and Keri holding her. Why her subconscious had put Keri there to care for her after being shot was a mystery. She rubbed the jagged scar on her upper arm, a constant reminder of the betrayal she'd barely lived through.

Her stomach grumbled, reminding her that she hadn't eaten last night. She searched one of the bags Wren delivered and pulled out a box of Cheerios. In the fridge, she found a quart of milk and silently thanked Wren for having put it in there last night.

She poured cereal and milk into a bowl and sat down at the kitchen table. As she ate, she thought of her father. She allowed herself to remember how it had been before her mother died. They'd been a real family. She couldn't have asked for a better childhood. But then, when she was sixteen, her mother was diagnosed with stage four breast cancer, and everything changed. She died less than a year later. Her father retreated into himself. He was lost and depressed much of the time, and many nights, he drank until he passed out. Over the following year, they'd grown apart, scarcely talking to each other.

In the intervening years after she'd left town, the only locals she stayed in touch with were Frank and her grandparents. They supported her through graduation from San Francisco State and the police academy. They even pinned her badge on her when she became a Haywood Police Officer. She owed them a lot.

A little before two o'clock, she pulled into the parking lot of Gerald Williams, Esq. The fog had lifted, and her headache was gone, but her mood was just as grim. She was not looking forward to finding out what surprises her father had left for her. What messes was she going to have to fix? What debts had he racked up? Frank hadn't been any help. He would never bad-mouth her father to her. They'd been friends since first grade.

Gerald Williams greeted her. His slim build and gray hair reminded her of her grandfather. They were about the same age. Taking a seat behind his desk, he motioned for her to have a seat across from him. "I'm sorry for your loss," he said somberly. "Your father was well-liked and will be missed by quite a few people in town."

She nodded but remained silent.

He cleared his throat and opened a file folder in front of him. "Let's get started, shall we?"

An hour later, Devin walked out of the lawyer's office and climbed into her Jeep. Her head was spinning. The meeting had been emotional, and she was on information overload. She leaned her head back on the headrest and stared into space. Her father's will was straightforward, giving her the power of attorney to manage his affairs. His trust laid out how his estate was to be handled.

Her father had no debt. None. The house was paid off. Same for his truck, boat, and credit cards. He'd left everything to her to do with as she pleased. There was also $250,000 from her mother's life insurance that he'd put in a high-yield savings account for her over a decade ago. Surprisingly, he had a $100,000 life insurance policy as well, with Devin as the beneficiary.

Pulling up in front of her grandparents' home, she sat in the Jeep letting her head clear. As she approached the front door, she could hear Mikey barking his head off, and she pictured him running in circles around the living room. She didn't bother to knock and walked in. Mikey was waiting for her, standing on his back legs, paws in the air, wanting to be picked up, and, of course, she obliged him.

"You're not spoiled at all, are you, little man?" she said, laughing as he licked her face.

"Of course, he's spoiled. He's too cute not to be," her grandmother said, walking out of the kitchen and wiping her hands on a dish towel.

Devin set Mikey on the floor and hugged her grandmother. "Hi, Grandma."

The older woman returned the hug and headed back to the kitchen. Devin followed.

"How are things going at your father's?"

Devin paused, not sure how to answer. "I saw the lawyer today. Dad left me the house and his boat."

Her grandmother nodded. "As he should."

"But why? He turned his back on me. Hell, he disowned me."

Her grandmother walked back over to her and hugged her again. "I know this can't be easy for you, honey." She returned to the pot on the stove and gave the contents a stir. "But if he didn't love you, I don't think he'd have left you the house and boat. He could have donated them to the Fisherman's Fund."

Devin's eyebrows rose. "The what?"

Her grandmother wiped her hands on her apron. "He set up a fund years ago to help injured fisherman, or the families of the fisherman if he'd been lost at sea."

"My father did that?" Her disbelief was clear.

Her grandmother nodded. "I think he was trying to make up for past mistakes." She turned back to the stove while Devin tried to process the new information. "How's the packing going?"

"No big surprises so far. Lots of memories. I've been going through old pictures."

Mikey barked excitedly as her grandfather entered the room. He leaned down and kissed Devin on the top of her head. "Hi, kiddo."

"Hi, Grandpa." She picked up the saltshaker and mindlessly rolled it between her fingers. "What should I do with my dad's things?" she asked without looking up. "I don't want any of it."

Her grandfather sat in the chair across from her. "Devin, it's an emotional time. Don't be in a rush to get rid of everything. Down the road you may wish you'd kept some things."

"You're probably right. But I can't sell the house with all his stuff still in it."

"Do you need the money?"

Devin nearly chuckled and explained the financials.

"In that case, there's no need to rush, is there?"

Devin shook her head. "No, I guess not."

Her grandfather smiled and grasped her hand, squeezing gently. "It's a process, kiddo. Take your time with it. Let yourself grieve."

A frown creased Devin's forehead.

Her grandfather held up a hand. "I know you don't think you need to, but you do."

Devin felt tears threaten, but she held them back and sat up straight. "I've got his clothes boxed up. Where should I donate them?"

"The shelter on Morro Street is probably the best place for that kind of thing."

"What about his collection of glass insulators?"

"The things they used to use on telephone poles?"

Devin nodded. "He's got at least two dozen in all colors and sizes."

Her grandfather thought about it for a minute. "Some of those may be worth something. I'd take them to Jim Stone. Let him have a look at them."

Devin's eyebrows scrunched together. "Keri's father?"

Her grandfather nodded. "After he retired year before last, he opened an antique and collectible shop on Main Street."

No one said anything for a few minutes. Her grandmother finally broke the silence. "Have you seen Keri?"

Devin looked over her grandfather's shoulder out the window to the backyard and shook her head.

"Have you seen anyone?"

"I met Frank at the boat. We're taking Dad's ashes out on Saturday."

Her grandmother took three bowls out of a cabinet. "I meant have you talked to any of your friends."

Devin turned to her grandmother. "I don't have any friends here."

Her grandmother put her fists on her hips. "Don't be ridiculous, Devin."

"No one wants me back here. It stirs up painful memories."

Her grandmother sighed and put her arm around Devin's shoulder. "Don't be silly. You know there are people here who care about you deeply. Your grandfather and I certainly do."

Devin felt a lump in her throat as she thought back to the last time she'd seen Keri. The day they'd been caught kissing.

Her grandmother softly rubbed her arm. "Why don't you give Keri a call? I'm sure she'd love to hear from you."

"I don't think so, Grandma. She probably still hates me, and I've already had a run-in with Bo as I was leaving the bookstore."

Her grandfather huffed. "That boy needs to take a good look in the mirror and get his act together. He can't blame everyone else for the mess he's made of his life. He needs to take some responsibility for the choices he's made."

"If you went to the bookstore, you must have seen Chris," her grandmother said.

"Yes, I saw Chris and his husband," she said. "And Melissa's little sister delivered some groceries last night. She said her parents are at their wits' end with Bo."

"I'll bet they are. He's been in a bad place for a long time," her grandfather said.

"Did Chris tell you about Liz Bell's book signing?"

"Yes. He invited me to come."

"Oh, good. You'll go, won't you?"

Devin shrugged. "I guess. I don't have anything better to do."

CHAPTER SIX

It was a beautiful morning. A few clouds kept the temperature down, and the breeze off the ocean carried the earthy scent of salt and seaweed. The harbor was quiet, wrapped in a mist that clung to the water's surface. The distant cry of a gull echoed somewhere beyond the fog.

Devin dipped the paddle in and out of the water with a steady rhythm, the kayak cutting through the water soundlessly, each stroke leaving gentle ripples across the glassy water. She inhaled as deeply as she could until her injured lung screamed in protest.

In the quiet, she let her mind wander. Thoughts of what could have been. She didn't fight them. There wasn't any harm in it, so long as she didn't start thinking "what might have been," was still possible. She knew there was no going back and changing the past.

Thirty minutes later, she reached the end of the harbor, turned the kayak around, and headed back. When she reached the dock, she pulled the kayak from the water. It took every ounce of strength she had to load it onto the roof of the Jeep, but she did it.

Blowing out a breath, she climbed in and headed home to shower before going to Flybridge Saloon.

When she opened the glass door to the bar, the smell of stale beer, and french fries cooked in oil that needed changing days ago, assaulted her senses. Flybridge had been her father's go-to place after a long day of fishing. He and his friends would spend hours slugging back the local 805 beer and recounting their day on the water, good or bad.

The last time she'd been inside she'd been eighteen, a week before her father caught her kissing Keri. Mac, the owner, had called her to come get her drunk and belligerent father. When she arrived twenty minutes later, she found him passed out in a booth close to the front door. Two of his friends dragged him to her car and wrestled him inside. When she pulled into the driveway, she tried to wake him. He grumbled and pushed her away, so she left him in the car to sleep it off. The next morning, she found him in the kitchen drinking coffee. He said nothing about the previous night, and she wondered if he really didn't remember she'd brought him home.

"Devin," a deep voice called from across the room.

It was Mac. His hair had grayed, and his face wrinkled, but his smile was as friendly as ever. "Mac, how are you?"

"I'm good," he said as he quickly crossed the room and wrapped her in a bear hug. "It's so good to see you." He let go but kept a hand on either shoulder, looking down at her. "How are you?"

"I'm good," she said, smiling. "The place looks the same, and you're as handsome as ever."

"Liar," he said with a laugh. "I'm old and tired." He motioned to a stool at the bar. "Have a seat. Can I get you something?"

She rested her elbows on the bar. "I guess it's not too early for a beer."

"805?"

She nodded.

"I'm sorry about your father. It was a shock." He set a beer in front of her. "I'm going to miss—"

"What are you doing in here?" a voice yelled from the far corner of the room.

Without having to turn around, Devin knew who it was, and he sounded drunk.

"Bo," Mac shouted. "That's enough. Behave or I'll throw your ass out again."

Devin turned to look at him. His clothes were wrinkled, and he needed a shave. His eyes were red and there were dark circles under them. He stumbled as he approached the bar.

"She doesn't belong in here." He pointed at her. "Why the fuck did you come back?"

Mac came around the end of the bar and grabbed Bo under the arm. "That's it. You're done for the day. Go home, take a shower and sober up." He pulled Bo toward the front door.

"You're kicking me out?" He tried to pull his arm loose, but Mac held tight. "What the fuck, Mac?"

"Devin has every right to be here." He opened the door with one hand. "And you're the one causing trouble. Go home and sleep it off." He pushed Bo out and closed the door. He shook his head and returned to the bar. "Sorry about that, Devin." He sat on the stool next to her. "That boy needs to get his shit together."

Devin lowered her head. "He still blames me," she said, her voice just above a whisper. "I'm sure he's not the only one who's not happy to see me back here."

"Don't be ridiculous. Absolutely no one blames you."

"Bo does."

"Bo blames everyone but himself for the sorry state of his life. Don't let him run you off."

She gave him a half-smile. "Thanks." She took a sip of her beer. "I actually came in to talk to you about buying a round of drinks Friday night. It's something my father wanted to do."

"That sounds like a fine idea, Devin."

"I asked Frank to tell all his friends. Hopefully, it'll be a good crowd."

"There won't be a service?"

Devin shook her head. "No. Apparently, he didn't want one." She took a large swallow of beer. "Frank and I will take his ashes out on the boat this weekend."

"Well, we'll give him a good send-off."

Devin stood and reached for her wallet.

"Your money's no good here," Mac said.

"Thanks." She returned her wallet to her pocket. "I'll see you Friday night."

"We'll be ready."

CHAPTER SEVEN

Devin lifted another box of her father's unwanted things into the back of her Jeep and wiped a hand across her forehead. She walked back into the living room and took in the worn-out couch, scuffed coffee table, and ancient television.

She collapsed on the couch, staring out the window into the backyard. The tire swing her father had hung from a twisted branch of a cypress tree on her eighth birthday moved in the afternoon breeze. Memories of her father pushing her higher and higher and the excited squeals that erupted from her eight-year-old self brought a smile to her face. Those days were the happiest she'd ever been. Her childhood had been perfect until her sixteenth birthday.

She'd come home from surfing. The waves had flattened out, and she cut the day short. After storing her surfboard in the garage, she came in through the back door. Her parents were in the living room, sitting on the couch facing each other, holding hands. They were both crying. She couldn't remember ever seeing her father cry.

"What's wrong?" she blurted out.

Ever since, she had divided her life into two parts: before and after her mother's cancer diagnosis. Her father's grief was so consuming he couldn't see how much Devin was struggling herself.

The gunning of an engine nearby pushed Devin back to the present. She picked up another box and headed for the Jeep. The roar of the engine grew louder as she walked down the path to the driveway. A familiar souped-up black truck crept down the street and stopped in front of the house. Bo stared at her from the lowered window, his eyes filled with hate. Then he gunned the engine and took off, tires squealing.

Devin looked up at the puffy clouds that filled the sky, and exhaled. She needed to wrap up her father's affairs and leave Morro Harbor as soon as possible, for everyone's sake.

The jingle of the overhead bell announced Devin's arrival at Antiques by the Sea. She smiled at how small town Morro Harbor was. She couldn't think of a single place in Haywood that had a bell chime a greeting when you entered. Walking further in, she hugged the box of her parents' wedding china to her chest and let her eyes wander around the store until they landed on a woman across the room. Her heart raced.

Keri Stone was standing behind the counter.

Rooted in place, all Devin could do was stare. Keri was no longer a skinny, awkward teenager. She was gorgeous. Her light-brown hair fell in waves over her shoulders, she had curves that weren't there in high school, and she looked confident, self-assured. Torn between crossing the room or fleeing, Devin remained frozen, pleading with her heart to calm down.

Keri looked up. Her brows furrowed when she saw who it was. "I heard you were back in town."

Devin pursed her lips and nodded. "I didn't expect to see you here."

Keri crossed her arms over her chest. "I'm covering for Dad while he runs a few errands." She walked around the counter and stood in front of Devin. "What's in the box?"

The sight of Keri walking toward her caused Devin's heart to pound. With a gulp, she clutched the box and struggled to regain her composure. "Mom and Dad's wedding china," Devin murmured, her voice barely audible.

Keri's expression softened. "I'm so sorry, Devin," she said, reaching out and touching her arm. An electrical charge surged through Devin. "Going through their things can't be easy."

Devin nodded. "No. It's not," she admitted, her voice thick with emotion. "I just want to be done with it and get out."

"So, you're not staying?"

Devin looked away. "There's nothing here for me."

"I disagree. But you have to do what you think is best for you."

"My being here dredges up memories people don't want dredged up."

Keri leaned her head to the side. "You mean Melissa?"

Devin nodded.

"You can't still blame yourself. It's been over ten years."

Devin's jaw tightened, and she looked down.

"You should have let that go a long time ago." Keri's hand lingered on Devin's arm.

"Easier said than done." Devin stared into Keri's eyes. "You should hate me," she said, her voice just above a whisper.

"I don't." Keri paused. "I'm not going to lie. What you did hurt, especially how you did it, and I was angry for a long time. But I got over it years ago. It took too much energy. It wasn't healthy."

As they stood in the quiet of the antique shop, Devin felt off balance, and it scared the hell out of her. The familiarity of Keri's presence dredged up emotions she thought she had buried so deeply they'd never see the light of day. Yet here Keri stood, in the flesh, reminding her of everything she had tried so hard to forget. The way Keri's hazel eyes sparkled with kindness, and the curve of her smile still made Devin's heart skip a beat, threatening to overwhelm her.

Devin's fingers tightened around the large box, the weight of it grounding her. She knew she couldn't let herself get swept up in the past, not when she was still recovering from being shot and Tracy's betrayal. But the pull was undeniable.

Swallowing her nerves, she forced herself to focus on the task at hand. She'd come to drop off her parents' china, not to confront her own tangled feelings. Steeling herself, she focused on the present. She squared her shoulders and met Keri's gaze head-on. "Do you think your dad would want the china?"

Keri's eyes softened. "Yes, of course."

"Good." Devin nodded, relieved. "I have a box of my dad's glass insulators, too."

"I'd be happy to take a look at them," Keri said, a thoughtful expression crossing her face. "I'm sure there are collectors who'd love them."

Keri took the box from Devin and stepped away. Devin stood there, her arms at her sides, grappling with her thoughts. She had spent so long, convinced that revisiting them would only open old wounds. But standing face-to-face with the girl, now a woman, who had once held her heart in the palm of her hand was confusing. A mixture of excitement and fear coursed through her. It was a feeling she hadn't experienced in years.

"Dad will be back in a little while if you want to wait," Keri said, pulling Devin back to the present.

"Ah, no. That's okay." She fidgeted from one foot to the other. "I'll get the insulators. I can leave my number for him to call me."

Keri's smile faltered. "Okay."

Devin exited the store and returned carrying another box. She set it on the counter where Keri was looking at the china.

"Oh, I almost forgot. Would you tell your parents, my dad's buying a round of drinks at Flybridge tomorrow night?"

Keri paused before answering. "Your dad is buying?"

Devin nodded. "Well, his credit card is."

Keri crossed her arms and leaned her head to the side. "Am I invited, or just my parents?"

Devin hesitated, searching Keri's face. "Of course, you're invited."

Keri nodded. "Okay, we'll see you tomorrow night."

Devin shoved her hands in her pockets. "Okay. I guess I'll see you then."

As Devin headed to the door, she could feel Keri's gaze following her, but she refused to look back. For now, she had to just focus on getting through the next few days.

CHAPTER EIGHT

By 7:15 Friday night, Flybridge Saloon was filled to capacity. Someone had ponied up a dollar for the jukebox and Willie Nelson pleaded with mamas not to let their babies grow up to be cowboys. The half dozen tables were full and several men, some she recognized, stood in small groups, talking and drinking beer. Keri's parents waved to her from a table in the corner. She squared her shoulders and made her way over.

Keri's father, Jim, stood and wrapped her in a warm hug. She didn't know what she expected, but it wasn't that.

"Devin," he said after he let her go. "It's so good to see you. Have a seat." He pointed to the chair next to Keri's mother.

"Thanks, but I have to talk to Mac," she lied. "It's good to see you both. Thanks for coming, I'm sure my father would've been happy to see so many of his friends here."

"His passing was quite a shock," Keri's mother, Judy, said. "How are you holding up?"

Devin shrugged. "I'm okay. Just trying to get his things in order and get the house ready to sell."

A familiar-looking man with skin the texture of leather walked by and patted Devin on the shoulder. "I'm sorry for your loss. Patrick was a good man," he said.

"Thank you." She forced a smile, but she wasn't in the mood to hear how much people liked her father.

The man nodded to Keri's parents. "Evening, Jim, Judy." He nodded at Devin and continued on his way.

Devin turned to Mr. and Mrs. Stone. "Who was that? He looked familiar, but I can't place him."

"Joshua Harper. We all went to school together." Mr. Stone took a sip of his beer. "He captained a crab boat until he lost a hand in an accident six or seven years ago."

"That's terrible." Devin looked across the room at the man. She noticed he kept the end of his left arm in his jacket pocket.

"Your father wheedled every single fisherman to donate the proceeds from a full day's catch, and business owners, twenty percent of a weekend's sales to a fund for Joshua. Believe it or not they raised ten thousand dollars. With that combined with the sale of his boat he opened a little bait and tackle shop. That's how the Fisherman's Fund got started."

She looked at Keri's father skeptically. "My father did that?"

He nodded. "He did."

Devin was at a loss for words. Kindness wasn't something she remembered her father had much of. She spotted an abandoned stool at the bar, thanked Keri's parents again for coming and made her way to the stool before someone else claimed it. She watched Mac behind the bar pull a pint of lager and hand it to someone on the other side. He stretched his back and glanced down at the bar. When he spotted Devin, he smiled and headed in her direction.

"It's a good crowd, don't ya think?" he asked.

Devin gave a nod. "It's nice that so many people showed up."

Mac nodded as he wiped down the bar in front of her. "What can I get ya to drink?"

She gazed at the bottles behind the bar and spotted the familiar green one. "A shot of Jameson."

Mac's eyebrows lifted. "You drink whiskey now?"

She shook her head. "No, I hate the stuff. But it was his favorite when I was a kid."

Mac grabbed the bottle and filled two shot glasses. "A few years after you left, he actually quit drinking whiskey." He picked up one of the glasses. "To Patrick. May he rest in peace." He clinked his glass against Devin's and they both swallowed the liquor in one gulp.

Devin grimaced. "Why does anyone drink that stuff?" Mac placed a glass of water in front of her, and she guzzled it down. "It's like drinking gasoline."

Mac laughed. "It's a quick way to forget your problems for a little while."

Or forget you have a daughter to take care of, Devin thought, staring down into the empty glass.

As if reading her mind, Mac laid a hand on top of hers. "It's no secret your father fought a lot of demons." He picked up Devin's empty glass and set it in the sink. "But he'd give anyone the shirt off his back if they needed it."

"I find that hard to imagine."

Someone called Mac from the other end of the bar. "I'll be back."

Another dollar went into the jukebox and Reba belted out an upbeat, twangy tune Devin hadn't heard before. She let her foot tap on the bottom rung of her stool.

"I never took you for a country music fan," a familiar voice said near her ear. Keri's pink grapefruit and orange blossom scent filled her senses and set butterflies free in her stomach.

She turned to face Keri. "You still use the same shampoo."

The man on the stool next to Devin stood and offered it to Keri, who thanked him and sat down. "Either I've learned not to mess with a good thing, or I'm too lazy to change."

"I like it."

"Then I'm glad I haven't changed it."

Mac reappeared and looked from one woman to the other and smiled. "Keri, it's good to see you. What can I get you? It's on Devin."

Devin shrugged. "On my father anyway."

Keri looked at Devin, her face expressionless, then turned to Mac. "A glass of chardonnay, please."

"I'll have a Guinness," Devin said.

"Coming right up."

"It's kind of ironic, don't you think?" Keri glanced at Devin in the mirror behind the bar and smiled.

"How so?"

"Your father buying me a drink."

A chuckle escaped from Devin. "He's probably rolling over in his grave. If he were in a grave."

Keri playfully slapped Devin's arm where she'd been shot. Devin grimaced and leaned away.

Keri's eyebrows knitted together in concern. "Sorry, I didn't mean for that to hurt."

Devin rubbed her bicep. "No, it's okay," she said without explaining, and redirected the conversation. "I hear you own a wine bar."

Mac returned with their drinks and hurried off to another customer.

Keri took a sip. "I do. It's called Wine Time."

Devin took a swallow of her beer. "Did you study viticulture in college?"

"I minored in it. My degree is in business. After I graduated, I worked in a handful of wineries doing everything from production and sales to managing a tasting room."

"I don't remember you ever saying you were interested in wine."

Keri laughed. "When we were teenagers, the only wine I ever tried was disgustingly sweet and probably very cheap. It didn't leave a lasting impression. My junior year, I turned twenty-one, so I took a wine-tasting class. I discovered that well-produced wines are a delight. So, I took more classes and ended up with a minor in viticulture on top of the business degree. And somehow, I did it in four years."

Devin lifted her eyebrows. "Impressive." She lifted her glass. "Here's to you." She touched her glass to Keri's.

"Your grandparents told me you finished San Francisco State with a degree in criminal justice."

Devin nodded but didn't say anything.

"Then what?"

Devin's forehead wrinkled as she cocked her head to the side. "Then what, what?"

Keri pursed her lips and asked, "Then what did you do?"

Devin guzzled the rest of her stout. "Oh." She paused. "I went to the police academy. After that, I got a job at Haywood PD."

"So, you're a cop?"

Devin rolled her empty glass between her hands. "Honestly, I don't know if I am or not."

"What do you mean?"

She turned to face Keri. "Do you want to get out of here?"

Keri locked eyes with her, took a leisurely sip of her wine, and nodded.

Devin signaled to Mac, who approached. "I'll be back tomorrow to settle up. And if Chris and Bill, or Ms. Bell come in, their appetizers are on me."

Mac flashed a smile, nodded, and hurried to the other end of the bar and another customer.

The sun had sunk below the horizon, and with it, the temperature dropped several degrees. Devin looked up at the night sky. Millions of stars sparkled like diamonds on black velvet. "I forgot how clear the sky is here." She zipped up her jacket and shoved her hands into its pockets. "There's so much pollution in the Bay Area that you can hardly see the stars."

"That sounds depressing."

Devin shrugged. "You get used to it."

They stood facing each other, neither knowing what to say. Keri broke the silence.

"Would you like to see the wine bar? It's open until nine."

"Sure."

They strolled along Main Street without talking, enjoying a comfortable silence, before Keri asked, "What did you mean at the bar?"

Devin stopped. "What?"

Keri looked up at her. "When you said you didn't know if you were a cop or not. What did you mean?"

Devin shoved her hands in her jacket pockets, looked up at the stars, then looked at Keri. "I was shot."

Keri reached out and gripped Devin's arm. "What?"

Devin glanced at Keri's hand on her arm. She liked the feel of it, warm and familiar. "Tracy, my ex, was engaged in a lot of criminal shit. I didn't have a clue. When I discovered it, I when to Internal Affairs. She and three other officers were fired. She avoided jail by testifying against them." Devin shook her head and looked back up at the stars.

Keri kept her hand on Devin's arm and waited for her to continue.

Devin looked back at Keri. "By going to IA I broke a cardinal rule, don't rat on a fellow officer. They all turned their backs on me."

"But you did the right thing," Keri said.

Devin gave her a half-hearted smile. "That didn't matter." She paused, forcing back tears. "One night I was on a call to a burglary in progress. When I got there the warehouse was dark. I called dispatch for backup, then entered the building. As soon as I did, someone started shooting at me. I was hit in the arm. The bullet went through and into my chest, punching a lung." A tear escaped down her cheek. "Not one cop responded. They let me walk into an ambush. If someone hadn't heard the shots and called 911, I might have died."

Keri wrapped her arms around Devin's waist. "That is really fucked up."

Devin's mind raced, part of her wanted to continue to let Keri comfort her. Keri's arms around her, her head on Devin's chest felt amazing. The other half of her knew it was a bad idea. She wasn't staying in Morro Harbor.

Devin took a tiny step back, breaking their connection. She immediately missed the warmth of Keri's embrace. "Yeah, it is." She wiped tears from her face. "I'm on medical leave. When I'm cleared...if I'm cleared, I'm not sure I want to go back."

Keri wrapped her arms around herself. "I don't blame you. I wouldn't."

Devin nodded. "I have a lot to think about. And on top of it, I've got my father's shit to take care of." She looked down the street and then back at Keri. "Let's not talk about it anymore." She forced herself to smile. "We were on our way to your wine bar."

Keri nodded, and they began walking again.

Two blocks later, Keri stopped in front of a glass door, just down from Chris and Bill's bookstore. Several couples sat at small tables inside, and two women sat at the counter. "This is it," Keri said, holding the door open for Devin to enter.

A woman behind the counter waved to Keri. "I thought you were taking the night off?"

"I am. I'm just showing a friend around," Keri said. She pointed to a bistro table in the corner, and they took a seat. "We do have a few beers for those with less discriminating palates," Keri teased.

Devin shook her head. "That's okay, I like wine."

"Great. Do you prefer reds, whites, or sparkling?"

"Reds."

"Okay, I'll be right back." Keri walked behind the counter and took down four wineglasses. She poured a few ounces of a light-red wine into two glasses and a darker red wine into the other two. Carrying two glasses in each hand, she returned to the table and set two of the glasses in front of Devin.

"That looked very professional," Devin said, smiling.

"Practice makes perfect, right?" She picked up the glass that contained a light ruby red wine. "This is a red blend from Camins 2 Dreams, a winery in Lompoc. It's women-owned, and one of them is the winemaker."

Devin raised her glass to her nose and breathed in. "Nice," she said, then took a sip. "I like it." She took another sip and set the glass down.

Keri smiled. "I'm glad you approve." She picked up the second glass. "This is a zinfandel from J Dusi in Paso Robles. Again, women-owned and a female winemaker."

Devin swirled the deep-red wine before taking a sip. "That's yummy. It would be amazing with dark chocolate."

Keri reached into her jacket pocket and took out a dark chocolate Hershey's Kiss, setting it on the table in front of Devin. "I remember how much you liked them."

Devin picked up the kiss and unwrapped it. "Still do." She grinned and started to put the whole thing in her mouth.

"Wait," Keri said, reaching out and pulling Devin's arm back.

Devin's eyebrows knitted together in a question.

Keri chuckled. "Take a small bite of the chocolate, then a sip of the zin."

Devin did as she was told.

"Slowly swirl them around in your mouth," Keri said, with a knowing grin.

Devin's eyes grew wide. "Oh my God, that may be the best thing I've ever had in my mouth."

Keri raised an eyebrow, and one side of her mouth curled into a seductive grin.

Devin's face flushed crimson. "That didn't come out the way I meant it."

"Oh, I think it did," Keri laughed.

CHAPTER NINE

The early-morning air was crisp and carried the tang of seaweed. Steam rose in wisps from the water in the marina and the glow of the sun peeking over the hills to the east painted the sky in muted oranges and pinks. The marina was silent except for the distant bark of a harbor seal echoing across the water.

Devin and Frank stood next to her father's boat as it rocked against the weathered wooden dock. The morning chill made Devin zip her jacket all the way up and pull her father's red watch cap over her ears. Without a word, she knelt to untie the mooring lines and Frank climbed over the side onto the boat, its hull creaking as he walked to the helm.

As Devin untied the last line and climbed on board, the engine hummed to life. Frank eased the boat away from the dock and expertly navigated through the marina and into the harbor. As they motored past the breakwater, Devin looked back at the disappearing shoreline. Snippets of her childhood flashed through her head—afternoons with her father on the boat, catching her first fish, campfires on the beach, her mother helping her roast a marshmallow, her father laughing at her trying to keep the marshmallow from escaping her carefully constructed s'more.

"Coffee?"

She sucked in the salty air and looked around. They were several miles from shore. Frank stood next to her with a mug of coffee in each hand.

"Thanks, I really needed this," she said, taking one.

Frank nodded, never taking his gaze from the sea. "This spot okay?" he asked.

Overhead, a seagull let out a loud squawk. Devin glanced up, watched it glide past, before turning to Frank. "As good as any, I guess." She handed Frank her mug and reached for her backpack, extracting the square black box that held her father's ashes.

A slight breeze blew from the west, so they stood at the stern facing east. The last thing she wanted was to have the ashes blown back on them. She removed the lid and, with Frank's pocketknife, sliced open the sealed bag inside, exposing the small pieces of bone and coarse sand like remains of her father. Without stopping to think about what she was about to do, she leaned over the stern and lowered the container as close to the water as she could. As she poured the remains into the sea, as if by magic, a rainbow of color appeared on the surface of the water.

As she watched the ashes float and gradually dissipate, she felt a pang of guilt for her lack of emotion. It seemed wrong somehow to be so indifferent to the passing of her father. Still, try as she might, she couldn't conjure up any genuine sorrow.

She leaned against the side of the boat and let the briny air fill her lungs. She felt a weight lift. It wasn't cathartic, but rather a sense of closure and letting go of the anger and disappointment she had held on to for nearly a decade. Maybe now she could leave the past in the past and move on.

She glanced at Frank. His expression was unreadable, but his eyes were wet with unshed tears. She placed the lid back on the box as a dozen or more pelicans silently flew in a V formation overhead. They filled her with a sense of freedom.

Half a football field off the starboard side, water sprayed twenty feet into the air. A gray whale broke the surface and just as quickly disappeared. As the boat bobbed on the water, they stood in silence, taking it in. Was it a sign? Her father saying goodbye? Or just a fortuitous coincidence? Devin turned to Frank. "Thank you," she said.

Frank smiled, his eyes still damp. "Your father was far from perfect, and I know he had a lot of regrets, how he treated you being the biggest one. But he was my friend for over fifty years, I wouldn't want to be anywhere else."

They stood there looking out to sea for a few minutes longer, both hoping the whale would reappear. When the wind changed and the water became rough, Frank asked Devin if she was ready to head back.

She smiled and nodded. "I'm ready."

The sun was sitting low in the sky when Devin pulled into a parking space a few doors down from Keri's wine bar. Main Street buzzed with activity. A cluster of people stood outside Flybridge Saloon puffing on cigarettes, and a line had formed to get into Harbor Coffee and Tea. Gift shops were doing a brisk business and in the art gallery next to the wine bar, a dozen or more people took in the current exhibit.

She paused on her way to the bookstore to steal a glance through the window of the wine bar. Every table and counter seat was full. Her gaze wandered until it landed on Keri talking to a couple at the counter. Dressed in a sheer white blouse and knee-length skirt the color of autumn leaves, Keri was stunning. Her hair was swept up into a bun, and dangly gold earrings drew attention to the curve of her neck and down to the vee of her blouse.

Caught in the moment, Devin's gaze lingered, only to be met by Keri's teasing grin. Heat rushed to Devin's cheeks at having been caught. With a mischievous curl of her finger, Keri beckoned her in. Devin pushed open the door and stepped inside. She hardly heard the murmur of voices and the clinking of glasses as she watched Keri approach.

"Hi." Keri leaned in and surprised Devin with a soft kiss on her cheek. Keri wiped a spot of lipstick off Devin's cheek with her thumb. "Are you on your way to Liz's book signing?"

Devin's smile faltered. "Reluctantly, yes."

"How about I go with you?" Keri offered.

Devin's brow furrowed as she looked around the room. "Are you sure you can leave?"

"I'm not working tonight. I just stopped in before heading to the bookstore," Keri reassured her.

A smile returned to Devin's face. "Well, if you're going that way, I guess we could walk together."

"Like two friends."

"Just like that."

Keri smiled. "Okay, let's go."

The sun had sunk lower into the water, intensifying the vibrant colors of the early-evening sky. Along the sidewalk, tiny fairy lights playfully twinkled in the trees. At the empty storefront between the wine bar and bookstore, Devin stopped. "What used to be here?" she asked as she peered into the darkened window.

"A little T-shirt shop," Keri answered sadly. "They didn't make it through the pandemic."

"That's a shame," Devin said before they resumed their walk. "What's going in there now?"

"Nothing, that I'm aware of."

"Have you thought about expanding into it?"

Keri chuckled, shaking her head. "I've got my hands full with what I've got."

Devin held the bookstore door open for Keri. "Just a thought," she said with a playful grin, and followed her inside.

As if by magic, Chris appeared in front of them. "There you are." He pulled each of them in for a hug. "Let me get you a drink." He led them past a display of Liz's book and to the rear of the store where Bill stood behind a makeshift bar.

Bill leaned over and kissed Keri on the cheek. "It's good to see you." He smiled at Devin. "Glad you could join us."

"Thanks for the invite."

"Wine?" Bill pointed to the bottles on display.

Devin chose the red and Keri the white. Bill poured wine into glasses and handed them to Devin with a wink. "Have fun, you two."

Before Devin had a chance to respond, Chris grabbed Keri's hand and guided them to the front again. Just as they passed by the counter, Bo Bailey stumbled in.

"You've got to be kidding," Chris said. "I have to deal with this before there's a problem." Chris stepped in front of Bo before he could get past the counter. "Bo, you weren't invited. You need to leave," he said in a low controlled voice so as not to disturb the crowd.

Bo, a head taller than Chris, stared down at him and tried to push past him. "Fuck that."

Despite the low lighting, Devin could see his eyes were bloodshot, and he reeked of alcohol.

The room fell silent, all eyes focused on the commotion.

Chris remained in front of Bo, blocking his way. "Seriously, Bo. You're drunk and I won't put up with it." He put a hand on Bo's chest, holding him back.

"Get your fucking hand off me." Spittle flew from his mouth as he shoved Chris's hand away.

Devin stepped closer, ready to help Chris, but not wanting to stir Bo up any more than he already was, she didn't say anything.

Bo glared over Chris's shoulder at Devin, then back at Chris. "You let that fucking bitch in? Did you forget she's the reason my sister's dead," he yelled, his rage barely controlled.

Chris held his ground, his jaw set. He held Bo back with a hand on his shoulder and pointed at the door with the other. "You know that's not true. Now leave."

Bo's fists clenched at his sides. "Don't you dare defend her." His glare never left Devin.

From behind Devin, Keri said, "That's enough, Bo. I'll call the cops if you don't leave."

"Fuck all of you." His eyes bore into Devin before he turned and stormed out into the night.

Chris turned back to the room full of people. "Sorry for the disruption. Why doesn't everyone find a seat and we'll get started shortly."

Devin looked at Keri. "He still hates me."

Keri raised an eyebrow. "It seems some people can't let go of the past."

Devin shook her head. "It's not the same thing."

"Isn't it? Aren't you holding on to the past? To Melissa? To your father's reaction to our kiss?"

Chris stepped between them. "How about we go say hi to Ms. Bell?" Without waiting for an answer, he grabbed Keri's hand and led them to the other side of the room where chairs had been arranged for the poetry reading.

Ms. Bell stood near a lectern in front of the chairs. "Devin, Keri, I'm so happy to see you." She reached out and hugged them.

Devin returned the hug. "Nice to see you too, Ms. Bell."

"Devin, it's Liz, remember?"

"I know. I'll try."

"Okay, Let's get this show on the road," Chris said. "Are you ready?" he asked Liz.

She nodded. "Ready as I'll ever be, I guess."

"Okay, why don't you all find a seat."

Devin and Keri took seats near the front.

A tap on the microphone drew everyone's attention to the small stage.

"Welcome to Rainbow Books everyone," Chris's voice boomed. "You're in for a treat tonight. Most of you already know Elizabeth Bell. She taught English for many years at Morro Harbor High School. Tonight, she'll be reading from her debut book of poetry, titled *Solitude*. Please welcome Liz to the stage."

The audience applauded as she walked to the microphone and opened her book to a bookmarked page. Glancing at the audience, she smiled nervously at a few faces.

"Good evening, everyone. It's so nice to see so many friendly faces," she said, then began her reading.

After reading a half dozen of her poems, Liz closed the book and answered a few questions from the audience.

"Okay," Chris said, stepping up to the microphone. "Liz's book is on the table at the front of the store, and she'll be at the table next to it for anyone wanting to have her sign it."

"What did you think?" Keri asked Devin, as they stood.

Devin absentmindedly ran her fingers through her hair. "I'm not a big poetry fan, but I liked it."

"Me too." Keri held her empty wineglass up. "Refill?"

Devin nodded. "Melissa wrote poetry," she said as they stood in line.

"Really? I didn't know that," Keri said, as they stepped up to the makeshift bar.

Bill refilled their glasses but was too busy to talk. They found Chris at the register ringing up sales, so they returned to their seats and watched the queue gathered near the front table, patiently waiting to talk to Liz.

After Liz talked to the last person in line she picked up a cup of coffee from Bill and glanced around the store. When she spotted Devin and Keri, she walked over and sat down. Perspiration dotted her forehead.

"Are you okay?" Keri asked.

Liz nodded, took a sip of her coffee and wiped her forehead with a napkin. She tugged at the neck of her sweater. "Is it getting hot in here?" She fanned herself with her free hand. "All of a sudden, I don't feel good. I'm...I'm having trouble..." She dropped the cup, coffee splashed everywhere when it hit the floor. She clutched a hand to her chest and looked at Devin, her eyes wide with panic. "I need..." She tried to stand, but her knees buckled, and she fell forward. Devin caught her as she slumped to the floor, unconscious and barely breathing.

"Call 911," Devin yelled as she placed two fingers on Liz's neck. She looked up at Keri. "There's barely a pulse."

Chris rushed over and knelt beside Devin. "EMTs and an ambulance are on the way, but it'll be at least ten minutes."

"She may not have ten minutes." Devin looked at Chris. "Can you get everyone to move back?"

"Of course." Chris and Keri began moving everyone away. Bill appeared and took control of the crowd, allowing Chris to return to Devin's side. "What happened?"

"I don't know. She said she wasn't feeling well and then she collapsed."

Keri knelt next to Devin. "How is she?"

Devin looked at Keri and shook her head. "Not good."

Devin noticed a faint blue tint on Liz's lips. "No, no, no." She leaned down and placed her cheek above Ms. Bell's nose, hoping to feel her breath. Nothing. She placed two fingers on Liz's neck and cursed under her breath. No pulse. She tilted Liz's head back, ensuring her airway was clear, placed her mouth on Liz's and blew in two quick puffs of air. She placed one hand on top of the other, interlocked her fingers and placed her hands just above Liz's sternum. Pressing down firmly she counted each compression. Her injured bicep screamed in pain, but she ignored it, letting her training take over.

In a flash her mind went to the beach and her teenage self, trying to save her best friend's life. Kneeling in the sand, the icy water lapping at her feet, frantically pumping on Melissa's chest. Melissa's lifeless eyes wide open.

Don't die. Please don't die, please don't die.

Come on breathe.

Please, Melissa, just breathe.

Please don't die.

God, please don't let her die.

She shoved the memory aside and focused on each compression, begging Liz's heart to respond.

Please don't die. Please don't die.

Breathe damn it. Come on, breathe.

Don't do this to me again. Please God, not again.

When the wail of sirens pierced the air, she felt a glimmer of hope. The EMTs rushed in. Exhausted, Devin scooted to the side to make room. Too shaken to stand she sat there watching as one of them continued CPR until the other attached AED pads to Liz's chest.

"Stand back." The paramedic held his arms out and pushed a button on the machine that sent a jolt of electricity to Liz's heart. Her body arched violently, then relaxed. "She's back," the paramedic announced, pulling the stethoscope from around his neck and removing the AED pads. The two paramedics carefully lifted Liz onto a gurney and rushed her out to the ambulance.

Keri reached down and offered Devin a hand up. Devin shook her head. "I need a minute."

Keri sat on a chair next to her and placed a hand on Devin's shoulder. "You saved her life."

Devin closed her eyes and leaned into Keri's touch, thankful for her reassuring presence.

"I—"

Before she could get another word out, a shadow fell over them.

"I heard the 911 call on the radio. What the hell happened?" a gruff female voice demanded.

Devin and Keri looked up to find Miranda staring down at them.

After Miranda left, Devin remained seated. Beads of perspiration dotted her forehead, and she clasped her hands together to stop them from shaking.

Keri sat beside her and pulled her close. Devin leaned in and rested her head on Keri's shoulder. "You okay?" Keri asked.

Devin shook her head. A small sob found its way up Devin's throat as tears fell down her cheeks. Chris and Bill locked the door, and slipped into the office, giving them some privacy. Keri hugged her tighter, one hand rubbing Devin's back. She didn't say anything, letting Devin get it all out. After Devin's breathing quieted, she wiped away the tears without lifting her head from Keri's shoulder.

Keri softly kissed the top of her head. "Do you want to talk about it?" she whispered.

Devin inhaled deeply and slowly let it out. Her brown eyes red and swollen, she sat up and turned to Keri. Keri reached for her wineglass and pulled the napkin out from under it, handing it to Devin.

"Thanks." Devin dabbed her cheeks and blew her nose. "It all came rushing back. I was on the beach kneeling over Melissa, pumping her chest, screaming at her not to die." She started crying again. She leaned forward and rested her head on the palms of her hands. Keri continued to rub her back but stayed silent. "I can't stay here," Devin whispered. "I just can't. It's too hard."

CHAPTER TEN

Devin woke to incessant ringing. She opened one eye, rolled over and looked at the clock on the nightstand: seven a.m. She hadn't gotten home until almost midnight. Miranda had demanded they take her through the events prior to Liz's collapse, pressing them for details. Afterward there had been her breakdown and sobbing on Keri's shoulder. She groaned and reached for her phone.

"Hello," she managed to whisper.

"Are you up?" It was Keri. She sounded irritatingly awake.

"I am now," she grumbled.

Keri laughed. "Sorry. I'm a morning person."

"I remember," Devin said, sitting up. "You used to call me before the sun was up, so I wasn't late for morning practice." She stood and stretched. "I don't have surf practice, so what do I owe this early morning wake-up call to?"

"I called Miranda this morning. She was completely out of line last night."

Needing coffee before she could get into a discussion about Keri's ex, Devin pulled on a sweatshirt as she headed to the kitchen. "I don't think she likes me." She chuckled. "Chris told me she's your ex."

Keri paused. "We dated for nearly a year."

"And you ended it," Devin said as she scooped coffee into the coffee maker.

"Yes. I did," Keri said, without explaining.

Devin filled the glass carafe with water, poured it into the back of the coffee maker, and turned it on. "And she didn't take it well."

"No, she didn't."

"If you don't mind my asking, why'd you break up?"

Keri paused. "When we started dating everything was fine. But after a few months she became possessive and controlling. She'd call me a dozen times a day. If I didn't answer she'd come by the wine bar or my apartment and want to know why. There was no way I was putting up with that."

"I'm sorry to say I've known cops like that. Domestic violence in law enforcement is a dirty little secret no one wants to talk about."

Keri sighed. "She really wasn't like that in the beginning, and for the most part she's been civil, at least in public. Until…"

Devin took a coffee mug from the cabinet next to the sink. "Until I showed up?"

"Yes, until you showed up."

"Did you tell her I'm leaving as soon as I can?"

"No."

"You should."

"You're right, I should. Anyway, she told me she'd talked to the hospital. Ms. Bell had a heart attack. They did an emergency angioplasty. She was lucky you were there and knew what to do. You saved her life, Devin."

Devin poured coffee into the mug. "Training kicked in. I didn't even think. Until…" She set the coffee carafe down and looked out the kitchen window.

"Until you flashed back to the day on the beach with Melissa," Keri said gently.

"Yeah." She took a seat at the kitchen table. "It only lasted a few seconds, but it really shook me."

"Has that ever happened before?" Keri asked, her voice soft.

Devin cradled her coffee mug, the warmth spreading through her fingers. She leaned back in her chair, looking out the window where sunlight spilled into the room, casting a golden hue over everything. "Not like this," she murmured. "It felt so real. Like I was right back there, frantic, pleading with her to breathe."

"You're not responsible for what happened to Melissa. You did everything you could."

Devin took a long sip of coffee, letting the rich flavor distract her for a moment. "If you say so."

"I do."

Devin closed her eyes, her insides twisting. "Okay, but I'd rather not think about it." She topped off her coffee, her hands trembling slightly. "I need to focus on clearing out the house, getting it sold, and getting out of here."

"You're going to run away again, aren't you?"

"I'm not running," she said. "I just can't stay here."

Keri sighed, the moment stretching between them. "I wish I could change your mind."

"Keri, there's nothing here for me but painful memories."

"Am I a painful memory?"

Several seconds ticked by before Devin answered. "No. You're one of the few good memories I have. That's why I keep telling myself to avoid you."

"You haven't done a very good job of that," Keri said, chuckling.

Devin smiled. "No, I haven't."

"That should tell you something."

"What should it tell me?"

"Maybe you shouldn't hold back?"

Devin sighed and pursed her lips. "I need to take a shower and get dressed. I still have a lot to do around here."

"Do you need help?"

"No. You'd be a distraction."

Keri laughed. "A good one I hope."

Devin swallowed. "One that would keep me from getting anything done."

"Okay, I can take a hint. But how about dinner tonight?"

Devin thought about all the packing she still had to do. "Maybe? Let me see how much I get done today. I'll call you this afternoon." Devin stood and looked out the window. "I'm really not very good at keeping my distance, am I?" she asked herself.

It was close to noon when Devin walked out the front door with another box of her father's things. An older Toyota Camry pulled up in front of the house, and Wren climbed out. There were dark circles under her eyes, her clothes were wrinkled, and her hair in disarray. She looked like she'd been up all night. As she got closer, Devin saw she'd been crying.

"Are you okay?" she asked.

Wren sobbed and shook her head.

Devin hurried over and embraced her, and Wren let her head fall onto Devin's shoulder. "What's wrong?"

Wren took a step back and wiped her face with the sleeve of her sweatshirt. "It's Bo. He's in the hospital. He wrapped his car around a tree last night. It's totaled."

"Is he okay? Was anyone else hurt?"

"He was alone, thank God. His injuries are serious, but he'll survive."

"Let's go inside." Wren nodded and let Devin lead her into the house. "Have a seat. I'll get you some water." Wren leaned forward on the couch and rested her head in her palms.

Devin returned with water and a box of tissues. "Thank you," Wren said. "The police were at the hospital when I left. They were waiting on his blood tests." She looked at Devin. "He was drunk." Wren blew her nose. "He was arrested two years ago for DUI, but they only charged him with a misdemeanor."

"Because of the wreck, it could be a felony this time," Devin said.

Wren nodded.

"How are your parents?" Devin asked.

"They were frantic at first. Of course, they imagined the worst. The thought of losing another child…"

Devin placed a hand on Wren's back and softly rubbed.

"Mom couldn't stop crying. When the doctor finally told them he'd be okay she was so relieved she nearly collapsed. My dad had to hold her up."

"How badly is he hurt?"

"One arm is broken and three ribs. He has a deep gash on his forehead, and a serious concussion. They want to do a full CAT scan to check for internal bleeding. The doctor said he'd be in the hospital for at least a few days to monitor the concussion."

Devin didn't say anything, letting Wren continue.

"The police said he'll be arrested when he's released from the hospital." Wren took a sip of water. "My parents will have to post bail. Who knows how much that is."

"Around a hundred thousand dollars, if he's charged with a felony," Devin said.

Wren stared at her, her mouth gaped open, her eyebrows raised.

"But they can go to a bail bond company. They'll want ten percent up front as their fee."

"That's ten thousand dollars."

Devin nodded. "And they won't get it back."

Wren shook her head. "Jesus what a mess. Haven't my parents been through enough?"

Devin folded her hands in her lap and looked down at the floor. "More than any parent should have to."

Wren reached out and put a hand on Devin's arm. "I'm sorry, Devin. I shouldn't have dumped this on you. It's not your problem. I should go." She got up.

"No, it's okay." Devin stood. "I'm here for you, Wren. I'm here for anything you need." She held out her hand. "Let me give you my number." Wren pulled her phone out of her pocket and handed it to Devin. Devin quickly keyed in her number and handed it back. "I mean it, Wren, call anytime."

Wren reached out and put her arms around Devin. "Thank you," she whispered, then walked back to her car.

Devin opened the refrigerator, the cool air hitting her face, and fished out a bottle of beer from a local brewery. She collapsed onto the couch and took a long swallow. She debated whether to call Keri as she said she would.

The thought hit her like a shot of adrenaline. The pull to see Keri was so strong, but she knew spending time with her wasn't a good idea. She couldn't let her feelings for Keri develop into anything other than friendship. Despite the tingle of desire whenever Keri was near, she told herself she should keep her distance. The nagging little voice in her head reminded her it would stir up feelings she wasn't equipped to handle. So why was she thinking about calling Keri and asking her to come over for dinner? It was just food and a movie, nothing in the least bit romantic, she told herself.

She scrolled through her contacts until Keri's name appeared. A picture of seventeen-year-old Keri filled the screen. Devin had taken it the summer before her senior year. They'd all gone to the beach, Devin, Keri, Bo, and Melissa. The memory made her smile. She recalled the surf, the seaweed's tang in the air, and the sand between her toes. She had desperately wanted to ask Keri on a date. She was pretty sure Keri liked her, but what if she was wrong? It would make things awkward between them. As they dried off, Devin had glanced at Keri, admiring how the wet sky-blue bikini clung to her body. Keri had caught her looking and winked, making Devin's heart race.

"What the hell," she whispered to herself. "It's just dinner." The phone rang once, twice. Her heartbeat quickened.

"Hello?" Keri's voice did nothing to slow her heart.

Devin's mouth had gone dry, and she swallowed. "Hi." She tried to calm down. "I was wondering if you wanted to come over here for dinner instead of going out. Nothing fancy, I could grill something or get a pizza." She wondered if her voice gave away how nervous she was. "Maybe watch a movie?"

"Like a date?" Keri asked, her tone teasing but curious.

Devin paused for a beat, her mind racing, not sure how to answer. "Umm, no? I mean…I don't know, Keri. Can we not classify it?"

"Okay," Keri laughed. "Let's have an unclassified dinner and movie night."

A grin spread across Devin's face. "How about six?"

"That works for me. I'll bring a bottle of wine," Keri said. "I'll see you then."

Devin disconnected and took a swallow of her beer, trying to convince her butterflies to settle down. "What am I doing?" she wondered out loud as she headed to the shower.

A few minutes before six, the doorbell rang, sending a jolt of nervous energy through Devin. She paused, wiped her clammy hands on her jeans, and opened the door. A smiling Keri stood there, stunning in a yellow sundress, and a bottle of wine tucked under her arm.

"Hi," she said. The gold flecks in her hazel eyes sparkled, and the tiny dimple on her left cheek was adorable. She held out the wine. "I hope cabernet is okay. It goes with both steak and pizza."

"Perfect." Devin took the bottle and motioned for Keri to come in. "I ordered a pizza. I hope that's okay."

Keri nodded. "Sausage, olives, and tomatoes?"

Devin let out a small laugh. "Of course." She set the bottle on the coffee table. "Have a seat. I'll get a corkscrew and glasses."

Keri took a seat in the middle of the couch, the hem of her dress inching up to the middle of her thigh. "It's a screw top," she said, letting out a soft laugh. "I didn't know if your father would have a corkscrew."

"Good thinking, he probably doesn't," Devin said, walking to the kitchen for glasses.

"How's the packing going?" Keri asked, looking around the room. It was bare except for the furniture.

"Not as fast as I'd hoped," Devin admitted, setting the glasses on the table. "I keep getting waylaid."

"What do you mean?"

Devin poured the wine, giving herself time before answering. "Just about everything has a memory attached to it." She picked up her glass. "Let's not talk about it tonight, okay?"

"Sure," Keri said. She held her glass out. "How about we toast to our 'unclassified' night?"

Devin's butterflies kicked it up a notch. "Perfect." She clinked her glass against Keri's. "To our unclassified night."

Devin took a sip just as the doorbell rang, and she got up to get the pizza. "Here or the kitchen table?" she asked Keri.

"Here's fine with me."

Devin placed the pizza box on the coffee table and went to the kitchen for plates and napkins. Handing a plate to Keri, she said, "Wren came by earlier. Bo was in an accident last night. He was drunk."

Keri's eyes grew wide. "Is he okay? Was anybody else hurt?"

Devin offered Keri a slice of pizza. "He was by himself, thank God. His truck was totaled. He's in the hospital, pretty banged up apparently. He's probably lucky to be alive." Devin placed a slice on her own plate. "What movie do you want to watch?"

Keri smiled. "*Thelma and Louise.*"

"What? We've watched that like a million times," Devin said, laughing.

Keri shrugged. "What can I say—it's a classic."

Something woke Devin from a sound sleep. The room was dark, except for the light from the muted television. The last thing she remembered was eating pizza and drinking wine with Keri as they binge-watched *Grace and Frankie* after the movie.

A soft snore nudged her to consciousness. Confused, she tried to sit up, but something held her down. She squinted into the dim light and realized the weight was Keri. She was sound asleep, one leg sprawled across Devin's hips, one arm flung across her middle and her head resting on her chest. A small smile crept onto her lips as she remembered their playful banter that had turned into not so innocent flirting after they'd consumed the whole bottle of wine.

Devin delicately moved a lock of hair from Keri's face. Her mouth was slightly ajar, and a soft snore escaped her lips. Her eyelashes fluttered ever so slightly. Was she dreaming, Devin wondered as she shifted, trying to find a comfortable position.

Keri stirred. The tip of her tongue peeked out and wet her lips. She blinked a few times, her face scrunching adorably as she looked up at Devin.

"Shhhh, go back to sleep." Devin leaned down and kissed the top of her head.

Keri's lips curled in a lazy smile. She closed her eyes and snuggled deeper into Devin's embrace.

Devin closed her eyes and pulled Keri closer. She forced herself to go back to sleep and not move her hand to Keri's ass. Her head told her not to go there. If only her body would listen.

CHAPTER ELEVEN

Three days after Liz's heart attack and Bo wrapping his truck around a tree, Devin approached the visitor's desk of the San Luis Obispo County Hospital. Her chest tightened when she thought about how many times she'd stood in this same spot when her mother was near the end.

"I'm here to visit Liz Bell and Bo Bailey," she said to the woman seated behind the desk. A plastic badge on her lapel announced she was a volunteer.

The woman entered the information into the computer and smiled up at Devin. "Liz Bell was released last night. Bo Bailey is in room 210." She handed Devin a light-blue VISITOR sticker. "Here you go."

Devin peeled the sticker off the paper and stuck it above her left breast as she walked to the elevator. She wondered who had picked up Ms. Bell and taken her home. Was anyone staying with her? Maybe Keri would know. They hadn't talked since the morning after they'd fallen asleep on the couch. Thinking about it made her smile.

When the elevator door opened, she entered the drab gray box and pushed the button for the second floor. The overhead lights of the ward were harsh and sterile, and the air smelled of antiseptic. Beeping sounded from several rooms as she made her way down the hall. Nurses in pastel-colored scrubs hurried from one room to another, their expressions focused and determined. No one said a word to her. They were all too busy to worry about who she was there to see.

The door to room 210 was open, but a pale-green curtain pulled across the entry provided a modicum of privacy. She paused to collect herself, unsure how Bo would react to seeing her. "Do this for Melissa," she told herself before pulling the curtain back just enough to stick her head in.

She glanced around the room. There were two beds. Bo lay in the one closest to the window, his eyes closed. The other bed was empty. Next to each bed was a small table on wheels on which a pink plastic pitcher and matching cup sat. Comfortable-looking faux-leather recliners were next to each bed. A football game was on a television bolted to the wall, the sound muted.

She turned her attention back to the occupied bed. Bo looked small, not like the angry, intimidating thug who had been threatening her. His greasy black hair lay disheveled on the pillow. A bandage covered most of his forehead and his left arm was dressed from his wrist to above his elbow. Surprisingly, he was clean-shaven. She wondered whether he'd managed to shave himself or if a nurse's aide had done it.

"What the fuck are you doing here?" Bo's voice was rough and gravely. She wondered if he had started smoking sometime in the last ten years. Melissa would have been so disappointed if that were the case.

Devin swallowed and stepped into the room, letting the curtain fall behind her. "I wanted to see if you were okay. If you needed anything."

He stared at her. "Don't pretend you care."

Devin pursed her lips. "We used to be friends. You, me, Melissa." The second the words were out of her mouth, she knew it was the wrong thing to say.

"Get the fuck out of my room." His eyes bore into her, his anger barely controlled. "And get the fuck out of town."

She raised her hand, her palm facing him. "Okay, I'll go. If you need anything Wren has my number."

He didn't say anything. His glare said it all. She pulled back the curtain and stepped into the hall. A male nurse stood just outside the room.

"He's one angry young man," he said.

Devin nodded. "You must have the patience of a saint."

"It's challenging sometimes, but I love my job."

Devin thought about the uncertainty of her career and her future. "You're lucky," she said, then turned and headed to the elevator. As she retreated down the hallway, she shoved her hands into the pockets of her jacket, still feeling the sting of Bo's words. "Get the fuck out of town." That was the plan, she told herself. The sooner the better.

When the elevator dinged, she sighed with relief that it was empty. She didn't need anyone to witness her threatening tears. She pressed the button for the ground floor and closed her eyes, willing her tears into submission.

As she exited the hospital into the chilly afternoon, she zipped up her jacket. She'd been inside for less than half an hour, but the temperature had dropped at least ten degrees, and dark clouds had moved in. As she walked through the parking lot, rain began to fall, the drops slapping the pavement as if sharing her frustration. She looked up, the rain hitting her face. "Why are you doing this?" she asked herself. But she knew why. Bo was Melissa's brother. The three of them had been close. She owed it to her best friend's memory to reach out to him. It's what Melissa would have wanted her to do.

It was close to three o'clock when Devin took the off-ramp to Morro Harbor and wound her way down Main Street. The rain had eased, and the sun was trying to break through the stubborn gray clouds. The shops were open, but the sidewalks were mostly empty, save for a few shoppers hurrying from one awning to the next to avoid the drizzle. As she drove past the bookstore, she waved to Chris, who was out front sweeping the wet leaves that created a slippery but colorful carpet on the sidewalk.

She pulled into a vacant parking space across from the wine bar, turned off the engine, and leaned her head back with a sigh. The bright yellow open sign hung in the window, but she didn't see anyone inside. Indecision washed over her as she debated whether to go in. Waking up with Keri snuggled against her on the couch, her head resting on Devin's shoulder and their legs tangled together had been the best thing she'd woken up to in years.

But she wasn't staying in Morro Harbor, she reminded herself again. She couldn't afford to forget it. Keri deserved better than someone who couldn't promise to stay. She'd hurt her once. She didn't want to hurt her again.

However, the pull toward Keri was undeniable, no matter how she tried to fight it. The voice inside her head muttered, "Don't do it, Devin. Don't do it." She knew she should ignore the growing feelings for Keri. They only complicated her reason for being back in town, and her plan to leave as soon as possible.

Yet, her heart was going rogue. It wouldn't let her stop thinking about Keri and what might have been if she hadn't run away like an immature child. It was a battle between her heart and her mind, and she felt trapped in the middle.

She closed her eyes and gripped the steering wheel tightly. She shouldn't do this. Hell, she couldn't do this. It wasn't in her nature to engage in a meaningless fling, and with Keri, it wouldn't be meaningless for either of them. Frustrated, she started the Jeep and pulled onto the street.

CHAPTER TWELVE

Devin sat on the floor of her father's living room. Her fingers traced the edges of an old cardboard box, its surface yellowed with age, the tape on the seams barely holding it together. She'd been in town for over a week and wasn't even halfway done. She promised herself she'd finish going through the boxes in the garage today. It wasn't like she was going to keep any of it, but she didn't want to get rid of anything without at least a cursory glance at what each box contained.

She pulled out a photograph—a day at the beach when she was about ten. Her father, dressed in a simple white shirt and khaki shorts, her mother in cutoff denim shorts and a sleeveless white blouse, smiled at the camera. Devin was in the middle, all smiles as well, her hair wild in the sea breeze. The three of them looked happy. Tracing the faces with her thumb, her chest tightened. She put the photo to the side, the warmth of the memory a temporary balm. She'd been so young and innocent back then. Her life had been close to perfect.

The next item was a small wooden box, the top adorned with hand-carved flowers. She opened the lid. Tears blurred her vision when she saw the delicate gold chain and the tiny "M," her mother's first initial, attached to it. She fingered the charm. For as long as she could remember, her mother had worn the necklace. She had asked her father about it after the funeral. He said that the hospital lost it. Why did he lie? Why had he kept it from her? She was sure her mother would have wanted her to have it.

She undid the small clasp, fastened the chain around her neck and held the charm in her palm. She sobbed as the anger, familiar and bitter, rose in her chest. Why had her father deprived her of this small connection to her mother?

She sifted through more items—old books, a dusty pair of his reading glasses, a flyer for her first surfing competition when she was fourteen. Each one seemed to pull her in a different direction. Some pieces of her father's life felt like an open door, like a chance to rediscover a part of him she'd forgotten. Others felt like chains, reminders of their fractured relationship.

She picked up a small picture frame, its glass cracked, and its edges worn, but the photo inside was clear. She and her father stood side by side on the beach, her arm around a surfboard, neither of them smiling. Grandpa Joe had taken it at a surfing competition a year after her mother's death. Her father had been drinking, and she remembered the smell of whiskey on him.

What had happened to him? Why did he push her away after her mother's death? He wasn't the only one grieving. She had needed him, but he had disappeared.

Devin closed her eyes, exhaling. This trip down memory lane wasn't productive. She wasn't sure if she was ready to let go of the anger, the hurt. She definitely wasn't ready to forgive her father. She stood and walked to the window, the sunlight streaming through the curtains. For the last ten years, it had been so much easier to hold on to the anger, to let it define who she was, then to move on.

Devin taped the box closed and looked at her phone. Three o'clock. Two and a half hours had passed. No wonder she was hungry. She explored the contents of the refrigerator. The pickings were slim. She grabbed a bottle of water just as her phone vibrated. Her heart sped up when she saw Keri's picture smiling at her.

She put it on speaker. "Hi," she said, taking a drink.

"Hi yourself," Keri said, her voice soothing. "I hadn't heard from you since Monday, so I thought I'd make sure you hadn't fallen down a rabbit hole and gotten lost."

Devin chuckled. "No. No rabbit holes, but I've been sorting and packing most of the afternoon and I forgot to eat lunch. Manny's Tacos are calling my name. Do you want to join me?" She crossed her fingers.

"You pay, I'll drive," Keri said.

"Great. It's a date." Devin's eyes grew wide. "Wait. I didn't mean…"

"Relax, I know what you mean."

Devin let out a nervous chuckle. "I need to jump in the shower really quick."

"Okay, I'll see you soon."

The attraction to Keri was like a magnet, and it rattled her. She wasn't staying in Morro Harbor, never mind the fact that she swore she'd never trust another woman with her heart. No, she was better off alone. It was safer.

She shed her clothes and stepped under the spray, letting the hot water massage the tight muscles in her neck and back. Her mind wandered to the sensation of Keri massaging her muscles and touching her body. She shook herself out of the fantasy. It wasn't a good idea to let her mind wander too far, regardless of what her body might want.

She shut off the water, reached for a towel, and heard the front door open and close. She must have forgotten to lock it. She cracked open the bathroom door. "You're early. I'll be out in a minute." Keri didn't respond. She wrapped the towel around herself and walked into the hallway, stopping dead in her tracks, her mind racing to make sense of what she was seeing.

Tracy, in skintight jeans and braless halter top, her hair dyed platinum blond, stood in the middle of the living room. Her gaze raked Devin's body from head to toe. The look on her face left little doubt in Devin's mind what Tracy wanted. This was her worst nightmare.

"Miss me?" Tracy purred as she took a step forward, her eyes taking Devin in like she was dessert.

It only took Devin a second to pull herself together, anger replacing shock. "What the fuck are you doing here? Get the hell out." She pointed to the door with one hand, clasping her towel with the other.

Tracy moved a few steps closer, the smile never leaving her face. "Come on, baby, don't be like that. Aren't you happy to see me?"

Clenching her jaw, Devin did her best to control her anger. "The fact that I have a restraining order against you speaks for itself. Now get the hell out of my house before I call the police."

In a split second, Tracy launched herself at Devin, wrapping her arms around her neck and forcing her mouth on Devin's. Devin put both hands on the other woman's chest and pushed her away, her towel falling to the floor.

The front door opened, and Keri walked in. Her eyes darted from Tracy to Devin, who grabbed the towel and wrapped it around herself.

"Am I interrupting something?"

"Yes." Tracy smirked as she took in Keri.

"No!" Devin insisted, wrapping her arms across her chest.

Keri tilted her head and looked at Devin. "You're busy. I should leave."

"Yes, you should leave," Tracy said, eyeing Devin and running her tongue over her upper lip.

Devin shook her head, flinging drops of water from her hair. "No. Please don't go." She glared at Tracy. "She's leaving."

Tracy reached for Devin. "But, baby—"

Devin quickly backed away.

Keri pointed her index finger at Tracy. "Is this the ex who almost got you killed?"

Devin nodded, struggling to control her rage.

"Baby, you can't blame that on me," Tracy said, pouting.

Devin clenched her fists tightly to her chest. "I absolutely blame you."

One corner of Tracy's lips curled into a smile and her voice lowered seductively. "Come on, baby. I saw the way you looked at me."

Devin laughed out loud. "That look was contempt."

Keri took a step toward Tracy, her expression hardened. "You need to leave." Her voice left no room for discussion.

Tracy reeled to face Keri, sizing her up before letting out a short, dismissive laugh. She turned back to Devin. "Let me guess, she's the high school crush you couldn't forget, isn't she?"

Devin glanced at Keri and berated herself for not checking the door before she got in the shower. "Who she is, is none of your business," Devin said, returning her focus to Tracy. "For the last time, get out before I call the cops."

Tracy's body tensed. Her gaze flicked between Devin and Keri. For a brief moment, her smile faltered, but she quickly replaced it with something more seductive. "Come on, baby, you don't mean that."

"Stop calling me that!" She turned to Keri. "I don't have my phone. Would you call the police?"

Keri nodded. "My pleasure." She stared at Tracy as she took her phone from her back pocket.

Tracy glared at Keri, her fists clenched. For a second, Devin worried Tracy might hurl herself at Keri and scratch her eyes out. But instead, Tracy uncurled her fists and looked at Devin.

"Fine. I'll go. But this isn't over." Her voice was ice-cold and laced with venom. Without another word, she stormed out, slamming the door so hard it rattled the windows.

Devin stood frozen, adrenaline coursing through her veins, her pulse pounding in her ears.

Keri stepped closer and reached out. Her hand covered the fading red scar on Devin's upper arm. "Are you okay?" she asked softly.

Devin, her throat too dry to speak, shook her head. Her mind spun. The weight of everything—the betrayal, the grief, the memories—pressed down on her. She closed her eyes and tried to steady herself.

Keri put her arms around Devin's waist and pulled her close. As if reading Devin's mind, she whispered, "I got you."

Devin, giving in to the embrace, let her head fall onto Keri's shoulder. "I know you do."

CHAPTER THIRTEEN

Devin stretched out on the couch and screwed the top off a bottle of water. The last rays of sunlight filtered through the window, casting shadows across the floor. A tree branch, whipped by wind against the living room window, was the only sound.

She pushed away thoughts of Tracy's shocking arrival the previous day and let in memories of her dinner with Keri afterward. It had just been tacos at Manny's, not very romantic, but it had felt like a date. It would have been so easy to invite Keri back to her house for dessert. But it wasn't really about dessert, was it?

A knock on the front door startled her. She hadn't heard a car, and she wasn't expecting anyone. With a groan she forced herself to stand. Her thighs burned, and she winced at the pain in her shoulder. Packing boxes all day was taking a toll.

She opened the door, surprised to find Wren standing there. She looked exhausted, her eyes were red. Devin's eyebrows furrowed. "Wren. Is everything all right?"

"Can I come in?" she asked.

Devin opened the door all the way. "Of course."

Wren dropped her purse next to the couch and sat. "Bo's been released from the hospital," she said, her voice hoarse. "He's got a court date on Monday. My parents put up their house to get him out on bail."

Devin sat beside her, close but not touching, her hands clasped in her lap. She didn't speak.

Wren leaned back and stared at the ceiling. "He's angry. At himself, at the world...at you."

Devin walked to the window, resting her head against the cool glass. "I don't know what to do, Wren." She paused. "If Melissa were here—" The words died on her lips. It was too painful. She pulled her shoulders back and turned around. "I'll go to the court hearing with you. If you want," she said. "If your parents are okay with it."

Wren's brows drew close. "First of all, my parents would welcome you. They don't blame you, Devin."

Devin cocked her head. "I'm not so sure about that."

"In ten years, I've never heard them lay any blame on you."

"If you say so."

"I do say so," Wren said. "But more importantly, I couldn't ask you to go to the hearing. This isn't your problem."

"You didn't ask me." Devin crossed the room and sank back onto the couch beside her. Silence stretched between them before Devin cleared her throat. "Melissa was my best friend, Wren, and he's her brother. He's *your* brother. I can at least be there for you and your parents. I think Melissa would want that."

Wren placed a hand on Devin's. "Thank you," she whispered.

CHAPTER FOURTEEN

Devin hadn't been up long when her phone chimed. She smiled at the picture of her grandmother and Mikey. "Hello, Grandma."

"Good morning." Her grandmother sounded wide awake. "We haven't seen you all week," she said, gently chastising.

"Yeah, I'm sorry about that. By the time I finish packing every day, I'm exhausted."

"I'm sure you're not eating anything healthy. Why don't you come to dinner tonight? And bring Keri with you."

Devin shook her head as she reached for a mug. "I'd love to come for dinner. But I don't think bringing Keri is such a good idea."

"Nonsense. We'll see the two of you at six o'clock." Her grandmother ended the call without giving Devin a chance to argue.

Devin poured coffee into her mug and took a seat at the table. She wished her grandmother wouldn't meddle in her love life. She meant well, but no matter what her heart wanted, staying in Morro Harbor was not an option. It wasn't like she could get a job with the police department. The town wasn't big enough for both her and Miranda in uniform. And even if there were an opening, Miranda would never hire her. Miranda wanted her out of town and far away from Keri.

She let out a deep sigh. The weight of leaving pressed heavily, heavier with each passing day. She took a slow sip of coffee, the warmth doing little to ease her tension. Was she making a mistake? Was she running from ghosts that only existed in her head?

She dialed Keri's number. It only rang twice.

"Good morning," Keri said, sounding chipper.

"Good morning." Devin took another sip of coffee before she continued, "If you don't have plans, Grandma asked me to bring you to dinner tonight."

Keri hesitated before chuckling. "Your grandma asked, huh?"

"More like insisted," Devin admitted, a small smile playing at her lips. "She's expecting you."

"Well, how can I say no?"

Devin chewed her bottom lip. "I don't want you to feel pressured."

"I'd love to see your grandparents. And you."

Devin smiled. "Okay. I'll pick you up at five thirty."

"Sounds good," Keri agreed. "See you then."

Devin stared into her coffee. Tonight would be fine, she told herself. Or not. Either way, there was no avoiding it now.

At five thirty, Devin pulled up in front of Keri's apartment over the wine bar. Keri in tight-fitting black jeans and a multicolored blouse, hair pulled back into a ponytail, waited on the sidewalk. Grinning, she slid into the passenger seat. "Hi," she said, buckling her seatbelt.

"Hi yourself," Devin replied, pulling away from the curb. "I hope my grandparents don't overwhelm you."

Keri chuckled. "I love your grandparents."

Devin grinned. "I love them too, but sometimes they don't know when to mind their own business."

As they drove through town, Devin was very aware of Keri sitting next to her—the way her perfume mixed with the crisp sea air drifting in through the open window. The attraction she felt toward Keri was growing stronger, and it scared her.

Her grandfather was waiting on the porch, Mikey yapping excitedly at his feet. "About time you two showed up," her grandfather teased as they stepped out of the Jeep.

Her grandmother emerged from the house, wiping her hands on her apron. "Keri, sweetheart, come in. Dinner's just about ready." The aroma of meatloaf and roasted potatoes filled the house, mixed with the scent of fresh-baked cherry pie.

"It smells wonderful," Keri said, as they walked to the dining room, Mikey trotting behind them, weaving between their legs before curling up under the table.

"I hope you like it," Grandma said. "Have a seat. Everything's ready." Devin's grandparents took their usual seats at either end of the table, Keri and Devin took the other two across from each other.

As Devin placed a napkin in her lap her grandfather focused on her. "How's it going at your father's place?"

She paused. "It's…going," she said vaguely. "There's still a lot to sort through."

He gave her a knowing look. "I bet. It's never easy going through a loved one's things."

Devin nodded, hoping he wouldn't press further. She glanced at Keri who winked at her.

"Speaking of sorting through things," Keri said, "I've been revamping the menu at the wine bar. I thought I'd have a female winemaker night."

"Oh, that sounds like fun," Grandma said. "Maybe we can get your grandfather to branch out and try something besides beer."

He laughed, and the conversation continued. Devin half listened, focusing instead on the way Keri's eyes sparkled as she talked about something she loved.

After enjoying her grandfather's amazing cherry pie, Devin and Keri said their goodbyes. Except for the radio, the drive back to Keri's apartment was quiet. When Devin pulled up in front of the wine bar, Keri turned to her.

"Do you want to come in for a glass of wine?" she asked.

Devin hesitated. She shouldn't. Every time she was around Keri, the lure grew stronger, and she wasn't sure she could keep things in the friends zone. But the look in Keri's eyes made her resolve waver. "Just one," she finally said.

Keri led Devin up to her apartment. It was an inviting, cozy space with warm lighting and shelves lined with books and bottles of wine. She poured them each a glass of cabernet and they settled onto the couch in comfortable silence. Devin tried to ignore the way Keri's knee brushed against hers or how soft Keri's lips looked in the warm glow of the lamp.

"You're quiet tonight," Keri said, tilting her head.

Devin stared into her wineglass. "Just thinking."

"About what?"

Devin hesitated. "What would have happened if my father hadn't walked in on us." She searched Keri's eyes. "Would we have had sex that day…that summer?"

Keri's lips curled into a smile, and she ran a finger along Devin's jaw. "We were horny teenagers, and you already had your hand under my shirt. I have no doubt that if he hadn't come home and found us, we'd have gone a lot further."

Devin set her glass down, and without thinking, without overanalyzing, she leaned in. Their lips met tentatively at first, then Keri's lips parted, inviting Devin to deepen the kiss. Everything around them faded away, leaving only the press of their lips.

Keri's fingers trailed up Devin's arm, sending shivers down her spine. She felt like she was poised on a precipice. If she wasn't careful, she'd fall.

Would that be such a bad thing? the voice in her head asked.

When they eventually pulled apart, Keri's forehead rested against Devin's. "I've wanted to kiss you from the moment you walked into my dad's store," she whispered.

Devin ran her thumb up the nape of Keri's neck and whispered in her ear, "Me too."

Keri shifted closer, one hand cupping the back of Devin's neck and the fingers of her other hand brushing along Devin's jaw. "I haven't been able to get you out of my head." Looking vulnerable, her eyes searched Devin's.

Devin traced her thumb over Keri's swollen lips. "Me neither," she confessed.

"Will you stay with me tonight?" Keri asked.

Devin knew she should say no, that she should walk away before this became something she couldn't walk back from. Before one, or both, got hurt. But Keri leaned in and kissed her neck, sending shocks of electricity to her core, and she moaned. She couldn't say no. There *was* no turning back.

"Yes," Devin whispered.

Keri raised her lips and Devin met her halfway. She'd worry about the consequences tomorrow. Tonight, she'd give in to what her heart wanted.

The first chime barely registered in Devin's mind, blending her sexy dream that involved Keri and her amazing mouth. But the second chime pulled her further from sleep. She groaned, reluctant to let the dream go until she realized she wasn't in her own bed, and that realization brought a smile to her lips.

Keri was wrapped in her arms, her back pressed against Devin's front, warm and soft and naked beneath the thin sheet. She smiled against the back of Keri's shoulder. Their bodies were tangled beneath the sheets, the warmth of sleep and something deeper keeping them close. She didn't want to move, didn't want to break the spell and let the outside world in.

Last night came back in flashes. The way Keri had whispered her name, the way their bodies had moved together, slow and unhurried, like they had all the time in the world.

The phone chimed again, and Keri reached for it.

Devin sighed and nuzzled the back of her neck. "Too early," she murmured.

Keri ignored her and looked at the screen. "It's Chris."

"What could he want this early?" Devin said, kissing Keri's shoulder.

"Chris? Is everything okay?" Keri asked.

Devin continued to kiss along Keri's shoulder until Keri threw off the sheet.

"What?" Keri said, sitting up quickly.

Jostled, Devin sat up too, letting the sheet fall to her waist. "What's wrong?"

Keri turned to Devin, her voice tight. "Someone smashed my front window downstairs."

"What?" Devin said, swinging her legs off the bed. She heard Chris say he'd have Bill get plywood, and Keri should call the cops.

Keri wrapped the sheet around herself and stood. "We'll be right down."

"We?" Chris asked.

Keri ended the call without answering and began grabbing clothes. Devin followed, pulling on yesterday's jeans and hoodie. Minutes later, they stepped outside into the chilly morning air. The town was still asleep. Soft pinks and oranges painted the early-morning sky, the ocean air was crisp, and a lone gull circled overhead.

Devin heard Keri gasp. Shattered glass from the front window lay in jagged pieces on the ground, a gaping hole where it used to be. Chris stood nearby, arms crossed, looking grim. Bill was next to him, holding a pair of work gloves. Chris turned as they approached. He looked at Devin, one eyebrow arched in a question.

"What?" she said.

Chris smirked. "You're here early."

Devin gave him a small smile and a shrug.

"I can't believe this." Tears pooled in Keri's eyes as she stared at the destruction.

Devin put her arm around her shoulder, pulling her in. "I wonder if anyone else in town was hit."

"God, I hope not," Keri said.

"I'll get a sheet of plywood," Bill said. "Shouldn't take long."

Chris put a hand on Keri's shoulder. "I'll get coffee. You both look like you could use some."

Keri gave him a small, grateful smile. "You're a saint."

Devin crouched down, picking up a large shard of glass. "Why would someone do this?" she said, looking up at Keri.

Keri didn't answer. Devin stood and wrapped her in a hug. Keri stepped back, wiped her face and called the police, then returned to Devin's embrace. A few minutes later, a black-and-white SUV pulled up to the curb. Before the door even opened, Devin knew who would step out.

Miranda.

An early-morning headache Devin didn't need.

Miranda's gaze swept over the damage before settling on Devin. Her expression didn't shift, but something flickered in her eyes. "Didn't expect to see you here this early," she said.

Devin crossed her arms. "And yet here I am," she said with a smirk.

Miranda's jaw tensed. "Wonderful. I think—"

"Miranda, stop. We talked about this, remember?" Keri said, her tone biting.

Miranda scowled at Devin then turned to Keri. "Any idea why someone would do this?"

Keri shook her head. "No, and it doesn't look like anything's been disturbed inside," she said, turning her attention to the gaping hole.

"So not a break-in. Just malicious mischief." Miranda glanced up and down the empty street, then back at Keri. "I doubt it was local kids. Most likely out-of-towners. They'll be hard to catch."

Devin crossed her arms, her eyes burning into the back of Miranda's head.

Miranda turned to look at Devin as if knowing Devin had been sending her death rays. Then she returned her focus to Keri. "I'll check with the surrounding businesses, see if their security cameras caught anything."

Chris returned, carrying a cardboard tray with four steaming cups of coffee. He took one look at the tension in the air and arched an eyebrow. "Oh, good. Everyone's still standing and there's no blood spilled."

He handed a cup to Keri and Devin, then offered Miranda one. "No thanks," she said as she walked to the SUV and took out a digital camera. She photographed the crime scene while the others stood and watched.

When she was done, she turned to Keri. "I'll let you know what I find out," she said and strode back to her vehicle without a word to Devin or Chris.

"Wasn't she a ray of sunshine," Chris quipped.

Keri rolled her eyes.

Devin shoved her hands into her pockets and wondered how a morning that had started with such promise could turn to shit so fast.

CHAPTER FIFTEEN

It was almost noon by the time they'd cleaned up the mess inside and outside the wine bar. After she and Bill secured plywood over the broken window, Devin had gone home to shower and change and was back at Keri's within the hour. The two climbed into Devin's Jeep, made a brief stop at the corner florist for a bouquet of sunflowers, and headed to Ms. Bell's.

Along with two others, the faded blue-and-white house sat perched on a high bluff overlooking Tidelands Park and the harbor. Those houses had stood there since the fifties, weathered by the wind and salty sea air. The setting was idyllic, and the view spectacular, with sailboats bobbing rhythmically in the tide and pelicans sailing overhead.

Devin pulled her Jeep to the curb, cut the engine and absently rubbed the scar on her bicep. Lifting and holding the large sheet of plywood in place while Bill secured it had irritated the injury even more than kayaking. Devin looked at Keri in the passenger seat, the bouquet resting on her lap. She could tell Keri was still shaken.

As if she could feel Devin looking at her, Keri turned. "Do you think she's up for visitors?"

"I called. She sounded a little tired, but she said she'd like to see us."

Devin filled her lungs with the briny air and stretched. The past week had been chaotic to say the least. First, the confrontation with Bo, then Ms. Bell's heart attack, Bo's accident, Tracy, and then last night with Keri. All of it while trying to resolve her father's affairs.

As they walked up the path to the front door, Keri slipped her hand into Devin's and Devin interlaced her fingers with Keri's. It felt nice—too nice. She couldn't let herself get used to it.

They stepped onto the porch, and Devin knocked. The door opened and Ms. Bell stood before them, smiling. She'd lost some weight, and she looked a little pale, but her eyes sparkled. "I'm so delighted to see the two of you," she said, pressing a hand to her chest. "Come in."

The cottage smelled of vanilla and books. A quilt was draped over the arm of a chair, and a steaming cup of tea sat on the coffee table. Sunlight filtered through lace curtains, casting delicate patterns on the hardwood floor.

"These are for you," Keri said, handing over the bouquet.

"They're lovely. Thank you," Ms. Bell said as she ran her fingers over the petals. "Come, sit." She motioned to the couch. "Let me put these in a vase. I'll be right back."

Sitting on the couch next to each other, Devin turned and smiled at Keri. "I'm glad we did this."

Keri reached over and placed her hand on Devin's thigh. "Me too."

"There we are," Ms. Bell said on her return. She placed the flowers in a glass vase on the coffee table. "Can I get you tea? Or coffee?"

Devin and Keri thanked her but declined.

Taking a seat in the armchair beside the couch, Ms. Bell looked at Devin. "They tell me you saved my life," she said. "Saying thank you doesn't seem like enough."

Devin shifted in her chair, brushing off the praise. "I'm just glad I was there and knew what to do."

"Nevertheless. You are a hero, and that's not hyperbole."

Devin chuckled. "Wasn't that a word you made us use in a sentence back in twelfth grade English class?"

All three laughed.

Ms. Bell tilted her head, as if sorting through old memories. "Do you remember Sarah Whitmore?"

Thinking it was a strange question, Devin blinked. "Sure."

Keri frowned. "I don't think I do."

Ms. Bell nodded. "She was quiet. Kept to herself. A talented writer, but painfully shy." She looked at Devin. "Your kindness saved that girl."

"What do you mean?"

"You were the only one who noticed when she stopped eating lunch in the cafeteria."

Devin shrugged. "She looked miserable. I just asked her if she was okay."

Ms. Bell smiled. "No, dear. You did so much more than that. You sat with her every day for several weeks, even when your friends rolled their eyes. And you brought her snacks when you noticed she wasn't eating. You even convinced her to submit one of her short stories to the school magazine."

Keri's eyes widened. "It doesn't surprise me."

Ms. Bell nodded. "She told me, years later, that she would never have had the courage to submit it if not for Devin."

Devin's brow creased, not knowing where this was going.

"She's published several books since high school." Ms. Bell stood and retrieved a novel from the bookcase. She handed it to Devin. "That's her first."

Devin read the title. *What No One Else Saw*. She glanced back up at Ms. Bell, who said, "Read the dedication."

Devin opened the book, thumbed to the third page, and silently read the few lines. She looked back at Ms. Bell. "She dedicated it to me?"

Ms. Bell nodded. "What you did for her may not seem like a big deal to you, but it changed her life."

Warmth spread through Devin. She'd spent so much of the last decade trying to escape her past, she'd forgotten the good things that had taken place here. "I can't believe she did that," she said, handing back the book.

Ms. Bell shook her head. "That copy is yours. Sarah asked me to give it to you if you ever returned."

Devin set the book on her lap. "I don't know what to say."

"You don't need to say anything," Ms. Bell said, returning to her seat. "Just know that people here *did*—do appreciate you."

Keri placed her hand on top of Devin's and squeezed. After a minute Keri broke the silence. "Speaking of books. I read yours."

Ms. Bell smiled. "And?"

"The poems were beautiful. A few of them brought me to tears."

"Thank you," the older woman said. "I'm so delighted you liked them."

"I've never been a big fan of poetry, but I read it too," Devin said. "There was one I really liked."

Ms. Bell's eyebrows lifted. "Which one?"

"'The Fisherman,'" she said. "How he keeps going back to the sea, even when it nearly killed him. It broke my heart."

Ms. Bell nodded. "Yes, that one is special. I wrote it to honor the local fishermen."

Devin stared out the window. Whether or not she wanted to, she couldn't help but think of her father.

"You know," Ms. Bell said, breaking the silence. "I always knew the two of you would end up together."

Devin's eyes widened. "What?"

Keri let out a laugh. "Ms. Bell—"

"Oh, don't deny it," she said, waving a hand as if brushing aside their protests. "I saw it back then, even if you didn't." She smiled. "It was only a matter of time."

Devin pressed her hands against her knees. "It's not like that," she said, her voice quieter than she meant it to be.

Keri's smile faltered.

Devin hesitated, but she had to say it. "I'm not staying in Morro Harbor."

Ms. Bell studied her, her smile fading. "Oh, Devin…"

"I don't belong here. Not since Melissa." She hadn't meant to bring it up, but once the words were out, there was no reeling them back in. "People here, they still blame me. They won't say it to my face, but I know they do."

"No, Devin, nobody blames you," Keri said, shaking her head. "It was an accident."

Devin let out a bitter laugh. "I was the one out there with her. I should have—" She broke off, looking away. The past was a riptide she had spent years trying to escape, but somehow, it always dragged her under again.

Ms. Bell's voice was soft, but firm. "Melissa made her own choice that day, Devin."

Devin clenched her jaw. She had heard those words before. It didn't make them any easier to believe. For a moment, no one spoke.

"My dad..." Devin looked from Keri to Ms. Bell and tried again. "That summer, after graduation, he threw me out. I'd told him I was gay." She skipped the part about him walking in on her and Keri. "He said he wouldn't stand for a child of his to be a queer." She swallowed hard.

Ms. Bell set down her tea. "Life has a peculiar way of bringing us back to the places we think we've left behind."

"It doesn't matter." Devin met Keri's eyes. "I can't stay."

Devin saw Keri look away, her shoulders slumped. She hated herself for causing Keri pain.

Keri's words were hesitant and unsure. "What if...what if this time, it's different?"

Devin frowned. "Keri—"

"No, just listen," Keri interrupted, taking Devin's hand. "You don't have to run, Devin. People don't blame you. Why on earth would they? And you saved Ms. Bell's life last week, and that means something. You mean something here. You always have."

Devin looked away. "It's not that simple."

Keri's voice was just above a whisper. "Maybe it is."

Ms. Bell smiled. "You've carried too much for too long, dear." She reached out, covering Devin's other hand with her own. "I wish you could see yourself the way others see you. The way your friends see you." Ms. Bell gave her hand another squeeze before releasing it. "Leaving won't make the past go away."

Devin forced a tiny smile. "Maybe, maybe not." Keri didn't argue, her face a mask. But Devin saw the way she bit the inside of her cheek, perhaps to keep from saying something she'd regret.

They talked for a while longer—about the town, high school and people they knew, and Ms. Bell's recovery. She assured them she was taking it easy and promised not to overexert herself. Toward the end of their visit Ms. Bell surprised them. "My mother passed away a year ago. She left me her house. It's a block from here. I've been renting it out, but I'm thinking about turning it into a bed-and-breakfast. For writers. It's a perfect location. The view is breathtaking."

"Would you sell this house?" Keri asked.

"I haven't decided what I'll do with it. Maybe rent it out," Ms. Bell said. "My mother's house has four bedrooms, so I could live there and still have three rooms for the writers."

They discussed the pros and cons of such a venture before Devin said, "We don't want to wear you out. We should go."

The three women stood, and Ms. Bell reached for their hands, squeezing them. "I'm so pleased you came," she said, her voice warm.

Outside, the wind had picked up. Devin smiled at the way it tossed Keri's hair around her face and made her cheeks pink. As they walked back to the Jeep, Keri reached for Devin's hand, lacing their fingers together. "I think she's going to be okay."

"I think so too," Devin said.

And for the first time in a long time, she thought maybe she would be too.

CHAPTER SIXTEEN

Early-morning sunlight streamed through the kitchen window, casting a warm glow on the table cluttered with empty to-go containers from her solo dinner the previous night. Drinking a glass of orange juice, Devin stood looking out the window when a knock on the door interrupted her quiet morning. She wondered why anyone would be there this early. For that matter, why would anyone be here at all?

She opened the door to Keri standing there, clutching a white sack.

"Hi," Keri said, grinning nervously.

Devin's brow furrowed. "Hi?"

"I brought breakfast burritos. From Manny's."

Devin's mouth watered as she reached for the sack. "Oh my God, you're an angel."

Keri smiled. "Can I come in?"

Devin stepped aside and motioned her in. A faint scent of Keri's citrus shampoo filled Devin's senses as she passed by. She reprimanded herself for being unable to stop her excitement at seeing her. "Would you like some coffee? It'll just take a minute."

"Sure, I'd love some."

"Have a seat. I'll be right back."

"Can I use the bathroom?"

"Of course. You know where it is."

Devin busied herself in the kitchen, preparing coffee and trying to push away her elation at Keri's unexpected visit. She carried the mugs into the living room, only to find it empty. The bathroom door was open. The light was off. The door to her old room was open, and the light was on. She set the mugs down, took a deep breath and entered the bedroom. Keri stood in the middle of the room, her back to the door.

"Keri?" Devin said, just above a whisper.

Keri turned to her. "There are so many memories."

Devin could only nod.

Keri took a step closer and looked up into Devin's eyes. She reached out and touched her cheek, sending a shiver up Devin's spine.

Devin sighed, torn between the past and the present. Leaning down, she found Keri's lips. Time stopped, and the world outside that room vanished.

Keri placed her hand behind Devin's neck and pulled her closer. Her lips parted and their kiss deepened.

Devin forced herself to end the kiss. She fixed her gaze at Keri. The longing in her eyes sent a shock wave to her core.

"I can't make any promises," Devin whispered as she ran her thumb over Keri's lower lip.

Disappointment flickered in Keri's eyes, but she nodded. "I know, but can we just have this? Just for a little while can we forget about everything else?"

Devin hesitated, nodded, and returned to the kiss, ignoring the real world for now. She lowered her hands to Keri's waist and pulled her closer. Keri's fingers tangled in Devin's hair.

As they pulled away, their foreheads touched, and Devin sighed, reluctant to let Keri go.

"The burritos are getting cold." Her smile didn't reach her eyes.

"We wouldn't want that," Keri said, blinking away a tear before it escaped.

Devin held out a hand. "Come on, let's eat."

CHAPTER SEVENTEEN

On Monday morning Devin walked into the courtroom, her pulse quickening as she spotted Bo at the defense table. His right arm was held closely to his body in a black sling, and deep-purple bruises marred his face. He was speaking in hushed tones to a woman in a dark blazer, whom Devin assumed was his lawyer. As if sensing her gaze, Bo turned, his expression shifting from neutrality to a hard, icy glare. Her stomach twisted, but she refused to look away. She had no illusion about where she stood with him. He hated her. Still, she was here. For him. For Wren. For Melissa. And maybe for herself.

A small wave from the front row caught her attention. Wren. Devin hesitated as she was seated next to her parents. It had been years since she'd seen them, years spent wondering how they would feel about seeing her again.

Her legs felt heavy as she moved toward them. Unexpectantly, Mrs. Bailey stood and stepped toward her, arms open. Before Devin could react, she was wrapped in an embrace so warm and firm that she was left speechless. Her throat tightened and she willed herself to keep it together.

"Oh, Devin," Mrs. Bailey murmured, her voice thick with emotion. "We've missed you."

Devin couldn't move, couldn't speak.

Mr. Bailey stepped forward and pulled her into a brief but firm hug. "Thank you for being here," he said, his voice rough.

Devin swallowed hard and nodded, not trusting herself to speak. She sank into the seat next to Wren, who offered a small smile and squeezed her hand before turning her attention to the front of the room.

"All rise," the bailiff called out. "Court is now in session."

Devin stole a glance at Bo, his back rigid. She kept her hands clasped in her lap as the judge entered the courtroom, her expression unreadable as she settled behind the bench. The bailiff called the case, his voice ringing through the silent room.

"The State of California versus Robert Bailey."

Moving stiffly, Bo pushed himself up from his seat. He winced as he straightened. Devin's eyes flickered over him, taking in the bandage on his forehead and the way he favored his right side.

The judge looked down at the file in front of her, scanning the pages before leveling a firm gaze at Bo. "Mr. Bailey, you are charged with driving under the influence for the second time in less than ten years. Furthermore, this incident resulted in an accident. Because of that you are charged with felony driving under the influence. How do you plead?"

Bo shifted his weight from one foot to the other, his jaw tightening before he spoke. "Not guilty, Your Honor."

Not guilty. Devin wasn't sure what she expected, but the words sounded hollow.

Bo's attorney spoke up. "Your Honor, Mr. Bailey understands the seriousness of these charges. He is prepared to take the necessary steps to address the underlying issues. He is willing to attend Alcoholics Anonymous meetings and take steps to maintain sobriety."

The judge studied Bo for a long moment. "Is that true, Mr. Bailey?"

Bo hesitated, just for a second, then nodded. "Yes, your Honor." Devin could hear the strain in his voice.

The judge made a note in the file and looked back up. "The court takes these matters seriously, Mr. Bailey. Luckily, you were the only one injured in the accident. I'm setting the next hearing for thirty days from today. And as condition of your continued release on bail, you are to attend a minimum of five AA meetings per week and provide proof of attendance to the court."

Bo's shoulders tensed. Devin wasn't sure if it was from the pain or the conditions of his release. Maybe both.

"In addition," the judge continued, "your driver's license is hereby suspended effective immediately. You are not to operate a motor vehicle under any circumstances until further notice."

Bo's lawyer nodded in acknowledgment, though Bo's expression remained unreadable.

The judge's gaze lingered on him. "I will allow you to remain out on bail pending your next hearing, provided you comply with these conditions. Do you understand, Mr. Bailey?"

"Yes, Your Honor," Bo said, his voice flat.

The judge made another note, then closed the file. "We'll reconvene in thirty days. Next case."

Bo shoulders relaxed and he turned to look at his family briefly before he followed his lawyer out of the courtroom. He limped, his injuries obviously causing him pain.

Devin watched him go. She didn't know what she'd expected, but she hadn't expected to feel sympathy.

Mrs. Bailey sighed and reached for her husband's hand.

"Well," Bo's father said, "at least he has a chance to get himself together."

Devin wasn't sure if Bo saw it that way. She stepped out of the courtroom and into the nearly deserted hallway. The air was stagnant, and the smell of pine cleaning solution overpowering. She almost collided with Bo.

She stopped herself just in time and froze. Up close, the bruises on Bo's face looked even worse—ugly blotches in varying shades of purple stretched from his temple down to his jaw.

His dark eyes flashed. "What the hell are you doing here?" His voice was low, volatile, filled with contempt. His knuckles were raw and bruised on the hand not in the sling, and he clenched it into a fist. "Why were you in there? With my family?"

Devin steadied herself, fighting the urge to flee from his radiating anger. She'd known that being here would trigger him. What had she been thinking when she told Wren she'd attend the hearing? "I'm here for Wren," she said, forcing the words out calmly. "And Melissa was my best friend. I know she'd want me to—"

"Don't." He cut her off. "Don't you dare say her name. Not here. Not ever."

The words landed like a slap, but Devin refused to let him intimidate her. She met his glare head-on. "I know you still blame me," she said, keeping her voice soft but unwavering. "But I loved her too."

Bo's jaw clenched, a muscle in his cheek twitching beneath the bruises. His breathing was shallow, barely controlled. "You shouldn't have come back," he growled. "You should've stayed gone."

Devin felt the familiar sting, but she pushed past it. "I'll leave as soon as I'm done sorting out my father's affairs," she said. "But your bullying isn't going to make that happen any faster."

His nostrils flared, and he opened his mouth to say something, but before he could, the courtroom doors swung open behind them. Wren stepped out first, followed by their parents. His father's gaze flicked between them, taking in the tension in the air.

"Is there a problem?" his father asked.

"No," Devin and Bo said simultaneously.

Bo's jaw worked like he wanted to say more, but he just muttered, "I'll meet you at the car." Without another glance, he stormed off toward the exit, his limp slowing him down.

"Devin," Mrs. Bailey said, placing a hand on Devin's arm. "Would you come to our family dinner tonight?"

Devin could think of a million reasons not to accept. "I don't think that's such a good idea."

"Bo will have to learn to deal with it," Mrs. Bailey said, her voice gentle but firm. "Please come. We should catch up. It's been a long time."

Devin glanced at the exit. She knew Bo would hate it. But something about the way Mrs. Bailey looked at her made it hard to say no. After a moment, she nodded. "All right," she said quietly.

Mrs. Bailey smiled. "Good. We'll see you tonight."

As the Baileys walked away, Devin stood rooted to the spot, dread threatening to overwhelm her.

CHAPTER EIGHTEEN

Devin stared blankly through the Jeep's windshield, her hands clenched tightly on the steering wheel, her thoughts a tangled mess. A headache was making its way up the back of her neck. But the thing that baffled her the most was that she had agreed to have dinner with the Baileys. Why had she done that? She rubbed her forehead with both hands. Maybe talking with her grandparents would help her sort things out. They had a way of putting things into perspective.

She shifted the Jeep into drive and headed toward their home. When she pulled to the curb in front of their house, she wasn't surprised to see her grandfather, garden hose in hand, soaking his beloved gardenias. A few feet away, Mikey spun in circles, chasing his own tail. The sight brought a smile to her lips and brightened her mood.

Her grandfather smiled when he saw her. He turned off the hose and walked over, his arms open wide. "This is a pleasant surprise."

Devin walked into his embrace, the smell of his aftershave welcome and familiar.

"Hey, Grandpa," she said, squeezing him.

"Bad day?" he asked, giving her a knowing look.

She sighed. "You have no idea."

Mikey let out a sharp bark and sprinted toward the house, his stubby legs working overtime as he darted through the open front door.

The house smelled like fresh baked bread and lemons. It smelled like her childhood and her shoulders relaxed. Her grandmother stood in the kitchen, an apron tied around her waist, a smile on her face. "Oh, it's you. I was just telling Mikey he had nothing to be so excited about, but I guess I was wrong."

Devin bent to scratch Mikey behind the ears before stepping forward to hug her grandmother. "Hey, Grandma."

"Sit down," her grandmother said, already moving toward the fridge. "You look like you could use some lunch." A few minutes later, a plate of chicken salad sandwiches was placed on the table, along with glasses of iced tea.

Her grandparents sat at either end of the table. "All right, tell us what's got you looking so down," her grandfather said, taking a sandwich from the plate.

Devin picked one up and took a bite, chewing slowly. "Bo's hearing was today."

Her grandparents exchanged a glance but didn't say anything.

"He pled not guilty which wasn't a surprise. Nobody pleads guilty at their first appearance." She explained the court's terms of his release on bail. "Afterward, we ran into each other in the hallway. He was so angry that I was there with his family. And he yelled at me to leave town again."

Her grandmother shook her head and hummed her disapproval.

"How did you react to that?" her grandfather asked.

"I stayed calm. I didn't want to cause a scene. I told him I'd be leaving when I was finished with Dad's affairs, but his bullying wasn't going to speed that up."

"Good for you," her grandmother said.

"Luckily, Wren and her parents walked out of the courtroom right then and he stalked off." Devin paused. "Then his mother invited me to dinner."

Her grandfather's brows lifted. "And?"

Devin rubbed her forehead. "I said yes. I don't know why."

Her grandfather leaned back in his chair, studying her. "How do you feel about going to their home?"

Devin stared at her half-eaten sandwich, her appetite gone. "You mean to Melissa's home?"

Her grandfather nodded.

"Confused, I guess." She continued to stare at the sandwich. "I don't know what they expect from me. Hell—I mean heck, I don't know what *I* expect from me."

Her grandmother reached over and squeezed her hand. "You don't have to have all the answers right now."

"What if dinner turns out to be a disaster?" Devin said.

Her grandfather shrugged. "Then you never have to do it again."

Devin let out a small laugh. "That simple, huh?"

"Most things are, if you let them be," he said.

She picked up her glass, rolling it between her hands. Maybe they were right. Or maybe going to the Baileys' was a colossal mistake.

Devin paused at the bottom of the porch steps, staring up at the house. It looked just like it had all those years ago, a well-cared for Craftsman with a wide front porch and a wooden swing that swayed in the evening breeze. It felt warm and inviting.

Before she could even take the first step up, memories crashed over her. Melissa sitting cross-legged on the porch, barefoot and grinning. Melissa running out the front door carrying her pink surfboard. Melissa laughing, always laughing.

Ten and a half years. That's how long it had been since she'd stood in this same spot. The Baileys had been her second family, especially after her mother died. Sleepovers, family dinners, game nights. Bo had always been a part of it. Before she could change her mind, she gathered her courage, climbed the steps, and knocked.

The door swung open, and Wren stood there smiling. "Hi." She pulled her into a hug. "Come in."

It all looked the same except for a new couch and recliner. The walls were the same color and family photos were still displayed on the mantel. Her eyes landed on a familiar one. Melissa, sixteen, frozen in time. Grinning. Reckless. Alive.

Footsteps approached from behind, and then Mr. and Mrs. Bailey were wrapping her in warm embraces. "I'm so glad you're here," Mrs. Bailey said. "It's been too long."

Bo walked into the room. He just stood there, arms crossed, his face unreadable.

Devin met his glare but said nothing.

"Dinner's ready," Mrs. Bailey said, breaking the tension. "Come sit, Devin. Tell us what you've been up to."

Over dinner, Devin filled them in. Mrs. Bailey gasped when Devin told them she'd been shot. Wren looked simultaneously fascinated and horrified. She admitted she wasn't sure what came next career-wise. What she didn't say was how lost and alone she felt. And she certainly didn't mention Tracy.

Bo didn't say a word, his face a mask. Minutes passed in polite conversation before Bo shoved back his chair and stood. "I need to go."

His father shot him a look. "Bo, wait. We need to work out a schedule for your AA meetings."

"I can drive you on Wednesdays," Wren said. "That's my night off."

"I can take you Tuesdays and Thursdays. Your mother can do Mondays and Fridays."

Without thinking, Devin said, "I can help."

Bo's head snapped toward her. "No."

Devin's back stiffened.

"Bo," his father warned.

Bo's voice was sharp, bitter. "I can't believe you invited her here, or have you forgotten she's the reason my sister is dead?"

The words landed with the force of a punch. Devin clenched her fists under the table, forcing herself to meet Bo's glare. Anger burned in his eyes, but beneath it, she saw raw grief.

"Bo, that's enough," Mr. Bailey said firmly. "Devin isn't to blame. You know that."

"Isn't she?" Bo scoffed, turning toward his parents, pointing at Devin. "How can you all sit here like this? Like she didn't—like it isn't her fault?" His voice cracked.

Wren flinched. "Bo, come on…"

Mrs. Bailey started to cry. "Bo, please don't do this."

Devin swallowed the lump in her throat. Nothing had prepared her for the sheer weight of Bo's words, for how much they *hurt*.

Bo shoved his chair so hard it almost tipped over. "Why the hell did you come back?"

"Bo, that's enough," Mr. Bailey snapped.

"No." Bo's voice dropped, low and cold. "I don't need her help." His next words came out like a knife. "Why couldn't it have been you who died?"

Devin felt like all the air had been sucked out of the room and the walls were closing in.

"Bo," Mrs. Bailey tried again, her voice wavering.

But Bo had already stormed off. The front door slammed, leaving nothing but shocked silence.

Mr. Bailey rubbed his hand over his face, looking drained. Mrs. Bailey's eyes were filled with tears.

Devin exhaled shakily, blinking back tears. She pushed back her chair. "I shouldn't have come."

"No, Devin," Mrs. Bailey said, reaching for her. "We *don't* blame you." She squeezed Devin's hand. "We never blamed you. It was a horrible accident."

Tears burned Devin's eyes. For over a decade she'd believed that because Bo had blamed her, so did his parents. "But Bo—" she began, voice raw.

"Bo needed someone to blame," Mrs. Bailey said softly. "You were the obvious target."

She understood Bo's pain. She felt it herself. It gnawed at her every single day. Devin wiped her face with her napkin and stood. "I should go." She forced a small smile. "Thank you for dinner." She looked at the front door Bo had slammed on his way out. "I meant what I said," she added. "If you need help, I'm here."

Mr. and Mrs. Bailey stood, wrapping her in a hug. "Thank you, Devin."

Wren walked her to the door, hesitating before opening it. "I'm sorry about Bo."

"You don't have anything to be sorry for," Devin reassured her. She stepped outside, the night air crisp against her damp cheeks. The weight of the last ten years was still there, but now it was a little easier to carry. As she walked down the steps, the door quietly closed behind her. She wasn't sure what came next for her, but for the first time in a long time, she felt like she might be okay.

CHAPTER NINETEEN

The sun had only been up a couple of hours when Devin yanked open the garage door, determined to make a dent in the last of her father's life. Dust motes and stale air greeted her as she wiped a hand across her forehead and took in the chaos. Cardboard boxes containing who knew what were stacked in a corner and tools sat haphazardly on shelves. It was overwhelming.

She had spent the last two hours sorting through everything, deciding what to keep, what to donate, what might have value at Antiques by the Sea, and what was bound for the dump. So far, the "keep" pile was the smallest. Her father had stopped caring about any of it, and she was determined to not care either. But every so often, an item would surprise her, dredging up a memory she hadn't expected. A small tackle box with her name written in Sharpie, a reminder of the summers she had spent fishing with him as a kid. A deflated soccer ball. A photo album filled with snapshots of birthdays, beach trips with her parents and a younger version of herself she hardly recognized. And there were the surfboards she'd turned away from after Melissa died.

By eleven o'clock, her back screamed in protest, dirt streaked her jeans, and she was fairly sure a cobweb was in her hair. The thought of a spider there too made her shiver. She was considering taking a break when her phone buzzed in her pocket. She smiled at the name on the screen. "You called just in time," she said, leaning against the workbench.

"Oh yeah?" Keri's voice was warm and teasing. "Are you having fun?"

"Only if you find sweat, toxic dust, and dead spiders fun."

"Hmmm, nothing like a dirty, sweaty sexy woman to make my day," Keri purred.

Devin barked out a laugh. "Is that what you call flirting?"

"Maybe." Keri's voice was playful. "Want to take a break and have lunch with me?"

Devin hesitated. The thought of sitting in a crowded café, surrounded by people while trying to ignore the memory of Keri's touch, wasn't very appealing. She didn't know what she and Keri were, and she wasn't in the mood to figure it out over a Cobb salad.

"What if we take my dad's boat out?" Devin suggested. "We could pack a picnic."

"Oh, I like the way you think. I'll make the lunch and pick you up."

"I need a shower, so give me half an hour."

"Do you need help?" Keri asked, teasing.

Devin swatted away the picture in her head. "That's a very nice offer, but I'm starving."

"All right, but the offer stands. I'll pick you up in half an hour."

"Deal." Devin ended the call, already peeling off her filthy shirt as she headed inside. She scrubbed herself clean as the thoughts of Keri and their night together filled her head. Keri's warm skin, her soft lips, the way she'd felt in Devin's arms, pressed up against her. It had felt so good, really good. She sighed. Keri was making it hard to think about leaving.

When Devin opened the door thirty minutes later, she couldn't stop the smile that filled her face. Keri stood there in skinny jeans and a tight-fitting black T-shirt that left nothing to the imagination. "Wow," she said before she could stop herself.

Keri smirked. "That good, huh?"

Devin chuckled and shook her head. "Come on, let's get out of here before I do something reckless."

They drove to the marina, where Keri dropped the picnic basket into the boat and slid onto the bench next to the steering wheel. Devin guided the boat out of its slip and into open water. The ocean stretched before them, shimmering under the midday sun. A few miles out, she cut the engine, and they let the boat drift while they unpacked lunch—sandwiches, fresh fruit, and a couple of cold beers.

"This is perfect," Keri said, screwing the top off her beer.

Devin closed her eyes and raised her face to the sun. "Yes it is." In the back of her mind, she knew this could be the last time she'd take the boat out. She pushed the thought away, not wanting to spoil the day.

"Do you ever think about that day?" Keri asked, her fingers brushing Devin's cheek.

"The day my dad walked in on us?" She let out a small laugh. "Yeah. Hard to forget."

"I wonder if we would've stayed together if he hadn't."

Devin studied her. "Do you think we would've?"

Keri shrugged. "Maybe. Maybe not. We were so young."

Devin turned to face her, brushing a lock of hair from her cheek. "I never forgot about you."

Keri's smile faded. "Me either."

Devin leaned in and kissed her, slow and unhurried. For a moment, the past and future didn't matter.

On the way back, a pod of dolphins surfaced nearby, leaping playfully in and out of the waves, and pelicans glided gracefully overhead. It was a perfect moment—one Devin wished she could freeze and make last a while longer.

Back at the marina, they climbed out of the boat and walked to the parking lot. Keri let out a groan. "Oh, come on."

Devin followed her gaze to Keri's car. The rear tire was completely flat. She knelt to take a closer look. There was a small hole in the side wall. "It's been punctured, maybe with an ice pick. It's not an accident."

Keri sighed, rubbing her temples. "Seriously? First the window, now my tire?" She looked at Devin. "Is someone messing with me?"

"I don't know, but it wouldn't hurt to call the police and have them take a report." Devin pulled out her phone. "I'll take some pictures while you make the call, then I'll change the tire."

"You don't have to do that. I can call Triple A," Keri said, leaning against the car.

"Babe, I have many talents, changing a tire is only one of them." Devin winked.

"Sexy and handy. You *are* full of surprises."

"More than you know," she said with a grin before turning her attention to the tire.

CHAPTER TWENTY

Devin shoved open the garage door and surveyed the space. She hadn't made much of a dent the day before. There was still so much to sort through. The events of the previous day still bothered her. Keri's flat tire wasn't random. Someone had done it on purpose. But why?

She pushed the thought aside and turned her attention to the garage and the tools. She'd call Frank to see if he wanted any of them. If he didn't, he might know someone who did. Then she thought about the boat. Boats needed maintenance, and someone to actually use them. Selling it was the logical thing to do. She'd add that to the list of things to talk to Frank about.

She turned to the boxes and crouched down near the closest one. Inside was an odd collection of her childhood clothing— swimsuits, soccer cleats, a red raincoat, the soccer jersey from her middle school team. *Why in the world had he saved them?* She placed the clothing in the "to donate" pile and moved on.

One by one over the next hours, she opened the boxes, sorting through her family's past. The work, though mind-numbing and

slow, was also therapeutic. The eighth box, however, set her back
on her heels. It was full of books. Some, her mother had read to
her as a child. Others were favorites she'd bought when she was a
teen. She pushed the box to the "to be donated" pile and turned
back to the rest of the boxes, which she worked through quickly.
Most went into the "donate" or "get rid of" piles. There wasn't
much she would keep.

She knelt near the next box and brushed off the dust. Melissa's
name was scrawled across the top in Devin's teenage handwriting.
Inside a picture of the two of them made her smile. They were
young and carefree, arms wrapped around each other, grinning
like they hadn't a care in the world. Under the photos were
multicolored notebooks. She opened the first and recognized
Melissa's handwriting. Melissa had loved to write, filling notebooks
with poetry and hopes for the future.

Devin flipped through one, stopping on a random page. Her
vision blurred as she read the words.

In the gloaming
silence grows
light fades
waves rush in
then rush out
taking with them all evidence you were ever here.

The words hit her like a wave, a surge of grief crashing over
her. She could see Melissa—young, tan, laughing as she paddled
out beyond the break, fearless.

She didn't know how long she sat there surrounded by ghosts.
Eventually, she decided to give the box to Melissa's parents.
Emotionally spent, she left the garage. She'd had enough. It was
time for a breather.

The sharp knock on the front door interrupted Devin's break.
It took what little energy she still possessed to cross the room and
pull open the door. Miranda stood on the porch, arms crossed
over her uniformed chest, lips pressed into a thin line. The late
afternoon sun glinted off the badge pinned to her shirt. She
definitely didn't have the emotional or physical bandwidth to deal
with Keri's ex.

"Chief?"

"Can I come in?" Miranda's tone was all business.

"Do you have a warrant?"

Miranda glared at her. "Seriously?"

Devin shook her head and motioned for her to enter.

Miranda walked to the center of the room, hands on her gun belt, and surveyed the space, taking in the stained carpet, the couch that had seen better days, and the scarred coffee table. To an outsider, it must look pathetic, and Devin felt embarrassed for her father.

Miranda's gaze returned to Devin. "You want to tell me why trouble seems to follow you around?"

Devin sat on the arm of the couch and folded her arms. "Can you be more specific?"

Miranda snorted, unimpressed with Devin's feigned ignorance. "First, the window at Keri's wine bar is smashed. Then someone punctures her tire."

Devin cocked her head to the side. "And?"

"And both incidents happened since you've been back."

Devin wanted to laugh at the absurdity of the accusation. "Do you seriously think I had something to do with it?"

"It's a hell of a coincidence." Miranda's glare was steady.

Devin raised an eyebrow. "Miranda, you know I was with Keri when both of those things happened."

Miranda's nostrils flared. "You coming back has stirred up a lot of things. Not everyone's happy about it."

Devin's jaw tensed. She looked at the ceiling, counted to five, then looked back at Miranda. "The only one who seems to have a problem with me being here is Bo Bailey...and you." She didn't miss the way Miranda's gaze hardened. And then it clicked. This wasn't about the vandalism. This was about Keri. About her and Keri. Chris was right. It was obvious Miranda still carried a torch for her.

"Miranda, I've told you I'm not staying in Morro Harbor."

Miranda stared at her. "You sure about that?" Her voice had an edge to it.

Devin hesitated. *Did she really want to leave?*

"We don't need any more trouble."

Devin gritted her teeth. "Have you checked the security footage?"

"Of course I have," Miranda snapped. "None of the cameras were focused on the wine bar. I'm still waiting to hear from the owners of the art gallery. They're closed this week for a vacation."

"When will they be back?"

Miranda glared. "Stay out of it, Devin. It's a police matter. And you aren't a police officer anymore."

Devin rubbed the scar on her bicep, fingers tracing the ridge of damaged skin beneath her sleeve. "Technically, I am. As I told you, I'm on medical leave."

Miranda's jaw tightened. For a second, Devin thought she was going to say something else, something more personal, but she didn't. Instead, she said, "Take my advice—finish up what you need to do and go back to wherever you came from."

Devin let out a small, humorless laugh. "Careful, Miranda. You're starting to sound like a two-bit sheriff in a spaghetti western. Next, you'll be ordering me out of town by sundown."

Miranda didn't rise to the bait. She glowered at Devin before brushing past her out the door.

Devin stood in the middle of her half-empty living room, reeling. She wasn't sure what to make of Miranda's visit. She turned, walked to the kitchen, opened the refrigerator door, and closed it. Miranda's words about getting out of town echoed in her head. She pulled out her phone and stared at the screen. Should she call Keri and tell her about Miranda's visit?

She tapped her fingers against the counter, her frustration mounting. Miranda might not have been seriously accusing her of vandalism, but she was making it clear—Devin's presence in Morro Harbor was unwelcome.

She tapped her foot, trying to shake her nervous energy. She couldn't leave Morro Harbor until she finished what she came here to do. But Miranda's message, however backhanded, wasn't wrong. Trouble had a way of finding her, and Morro Harbor was proving no different.

Her phone buzzed in her hand, the sharp vibration making her jump. A text from Chris. *Are you and Keri free for dinner?*

Devin hesitated, then typed back: *I'll have to call and ask her.*

Chris's reply came quickly. *No need, I already did. See you at six.* He followed with a smiley face.

She shoved her phone into her pocket and glanced toward the window, where the sun was dipping lower in the sky. She fingered her mother's charm around her neck. Miranda might want her gone, but in that moment, Devin decided she wasn't ready to leave just yet.

Devin stood in front of the wine bar, hands tucked into the pockets of her black jeans as she watched the last hints of sunset fade into the ocean. She'd thrown on a red pullover sweater, comfortable and warm, but the moment Keri stepped out onto the sidewalk, she felt underdressed.

Keri looked stunning in a multicolored skirt that swayed around her legs and a soft, flowing blouse that caught the evening breeze. She'd pulled her hair back in a perfect French braid that showcased the delicate arch of her cheekbones, and she wore just a hint of makeup.

"Hi," Keri said with a smile.

Devin swallowed, aware she'd been staring. "You look amazing."

Keri's eyes sparkled. "Thanks. You look good in red."

Devin chuckled and shook her head. But before she could respond, Keri looped her arm through hers and gestured down the street. "Come on, we don't want to keep the guys waiting."

The scent of the ocean hung in the cool night air as they walked the short distance to the narrow staircase up to Chris and Bill's apartment above the bookstore. Devin let Keri go first, trying very hard not to admire how Keri's skirt moved across her ass with each step.

Chris swung the door open before they could knock. "Perfect timing! Wines are already poured," he said as he pulled each woman in for a hug. The apartment had a similar layout to Keri's, but where hers was warm and inviting, Chris and Bill's space burst with bright colors and local artwork.

Bill, already holding a glass of red wine, grinned from the kitchen. "Make yourselves at home. Dinner's almost ready."

Devin took a seat on the couch beside Keri, accepting a glass from Chris. She took a sip, savoring the bold, earthy taste. "This is good."

Chris nodded, taking a seat across from them. "It should be— it's J Dusi."

Bill came and sat next to Chris. "So, the bookstore was busy today, and Ms. Bell came in."

"We visited her Saturday. I'm glad she's getting out," Keri said. "How did she seem?"

"Good," Bill assured her. "Moving a little slow, but she was in good spirits. She told me her cardiologist wants her walking at least a mile every day."

"That's great news," Keri said, her relief clear.

Devin nodded. "She told us she may turn her mother's house into a B&B."

"Interesting," Chris said.

Keri lifted her glass in an impromptu toast. "To Ms. Bell."

They all echoed the sentiment before taking another sip.

"I've been thinking," Keri said, glancing from Chris to Bill. "I want to start a female winemaker night once a month. I want to showcase women in the industry."

Chris beamed. "That's a great idea. You should do a queer winemaker night too."

"Absolutely," she said. "There are so many incredible LGBTQ+ winemakers who deserve the spotlight."

Devin, quiet for most of the conversation, set her glass down. "Miranda showed up at my place today."

Chris and Bill both made a face, but Keri sat up straighter.

Devin let out a dry laugh. "She insinuated that I had something to do with the vandalism."

"That's ridiculous, you were with me when both those things happened," Keri said.

"Yeah, I reminded her of that. Then she strongly recommended I leave town sooner rather than later."

Keri shook her head, her fingers tightening around her glass. "What's wrong with that woman? I've talked to her once already about how she treats you. I'm going to—"

Bill clapped his hands together. "Let's eat. I made salmon with lemon dill sauce, pilaf, and a salad."

Devin turned to him, grateful for the change in subject. "That sounds great, I'm starving."

Chris laughed as they all made their way to the table. The meal was as delicious as promised, and the conversation flowed easily. They talked about upcoming bookstore events, new wines Keri wanted to introduce at the bar, and the latest town gossip—most of it harmless, some of it eyebrow-raising.

By the time they finished, Devin felt relaxed. She hadn't realized how much she needed a night like this—good food, good company, and a reminder that not everything in her life had to feel so complicated.

As they said their goodbyes, Devin fell into step beside Keri. The street was quiet—no cars, or tourists. The soft glow of the streetlights cast long shadows across the pavement. When they reached the stairs to Keri's apartment, Keri turned to face her.

"Do you want to come up?"

Devin held her gaze for a moment and smiled. "I do."

Keri's lips curved into a knowing grin, and she reached for Devin's hand. "Follow me."

CHAPTER TWENTY-ONE

Sunlight poured into the room through the white crepe curtains. Feeling the warmth on her face, Devin stirred. The sheets were cool against her bare skin, the scent of citrus and something distinctly Keri wrapping around her. She stretched, rolling onto her side, only to find Keri looking at her.

Keri rested on one elbow, her hair disheveled, a warm, amused look in her eyes.

"Were you watching me sleep?" Devin murmured.

Keri smiled. "Maybe."

Devin reached up, brushing a stray lock from Keri's face. Keri leaned into the touch. Without thinking, Devin closed the distance, pressing her lips to Keri's. Keri responded instantly, her hand sliding up Devin's arm, fingers tracing over bare skin, sending sparks deep in Devin's core.

They kissed slowly at first, savoring each other, then with more urgency. Keri rolled on top of Devin, pressing their bodies together, her hands exploring, her mouth leaving a trail of heat down Devin's neck. Devin arched into her touch, a moan escaping her lips. The rest of the world faded away.

The hot water felt good against Devin's sore muscles. She leaned her head forward, letting the pulsing water massage her shoulders. She could still feel Keri's touch, the imprint of her lips on her skin. A satisfied smile tugged at her lips. She wasn't sure where this thing with Keri was going, but right now, she didn't care.

By the time she had toweled off, Keri was dressed and waiting by the door, looking gorgeous in a purple sweater and jeans.

"Ready for breakfast?" Keri asked, her lips curved into a smile.

Devin pulled on her shoes and nodded. "Starving."

Dorn's Coffee Shop was bustling. They slid into a booth by the window, the view of the harbor spread out before them. The morning sun danced off the water, where otters and harbor seals bobbed in the outgoing tide. A few small boats moved lazily across the waves, the scent of salt and coffee mingling in the air.

Devin sipped her coffee, watching Keri stir sugar into hers. It was easy between them, comfortable, like they'd been doing it for years instead of something new and uncertain.

"I'm so glad Ms. Bell is doing okay," Devin said, setting her cup down.

"Me too. I might check in on her this afternoon." Keri hesitated before continuing, "I'm so sorry about Miranda."

Devin sighed. "It's not your fault."

Keri stared into her coffee cup. "It kinda is." She looked up at Devin. "It's been a year, why can't she let it go?"

Devin smiled and reached across the table, covering Keri's hand with her own. "You're a hard one to let go of."

Keri flipped her palm up, intertwining their fingers. "There's a dinner and silent auction for the Fisherman's Fund on Saturday. I was wondering if you'd want to go with me?"

Devin grinned. "Are you asking me on a date?"

Keri rolled her eyes, but her smile betrayed her. "Maybe."

Devin squeezed her hand. "I'd love to go."

Keri opened her mouth to say something else when Devin's phone buzzed against the table. She glanced at the screen. "Grandma? What's wrong?"

Her grandmother's voice was rushed and sounded frantic. "It's Grandpa. He was cleaning the gutters and fell off the ladder. He hit his head, Devin." Her grandmother's voice cracked. "We're in the ambulance on the way to the hospital."

"I'm coming," Devin said, reaching for her keys. "I'll meet you there." She disconnected and scooted out of the booth. "Grandpa fell off a ladder," she said. "I have to go."

Keri stood. "I'm going with you."

"You don't have to—"

"I'm coming with you," Keri said firmly, tossing cash on the table. Keri held out her hand. "Let me drive."

Devin looked at her questioningly.

"You're not in any shape to drive, and it won't do your grandparents any good if we don't make it there in one piece."

Devin nodded and handed over the keys. "You're right."

As they neared the emergency room, the automatic doors slid open, and she was hit with the sharp smell of antiseptic. The fluorescent lights cast everything in a cold, sterile glow. Her fingers tightened around Keri's. As they stepped inside, Devin scanned the waiting room. The number of people there surprised her. In the far corner, a young mother rocked a crying toddler against her chest. A man in obvious pain held a bloodied towel to his head, his knee bouncing nervously. An elderly woman sat in the back of the room, her head bowed, her lips moving in silent prayer. They were only a few of the two dozen or more people waiting to be seen.

Then she saw her grandmother. She sat slumped in an uncomfortable plastic chair, her shoulders shaking, her face buried in her hands. She looked so small and fragile.

"Grandma," Devin said, her voice unsteady. She hurried over and knelt beside her.

Her grandmother lowered her hands, her face damp. She reached out, grasping onto Devin's arm, as if Devin were a life preserver. "I'm so worried, Devin."

Devin swallowed hard, willing herself to stay steady. "It's okay. I'm here." Why did she say it was okay? She didn't know if it was or ever would be.

Keri moved beside her, her hand resting at the small of Devin's back, grounding her.

Her grandmother's lips trembled. "They took him for an MRI. He hasn't woken up since the fall."

Devin clenched her jaw, forcing down her panic. "Are there any other injuries?"

"A broken arm," her grandmother said, voice cracking. "But the doctors are more worried about his head." She covered her mouth with her hand, a sob escaping. "He was cleaning the gutter. I told him to leave it, that we'd hire someone. But you know your grandpa."

Devin bit the inside of her cheek, fighting to keep herself together. She held her grandmother close and surveyed the room. She'd been here before. Ten years ago. Devin remembered standing in this very room, Melissa's mother hysterical, her father trying to comfort her, and Bo furious, screaming at her that it was all her fault.

Keri sat down on the other side of Devin's grandmother and rubbed slow circles on the older woman's back. "Can I get you some water? Tea? Anything?"

Her grandmother shook her head. "No thank you, dear."

Keri nodded, staying close, offering silent comfort.

Devin wanted nothing more than to collapse into Keri and be held by her. But she couldn't. Not yet. Instead, she sat beside her grandmother, holding her hands. "He's strong," she whispered. "He's going to be okay."

Her grandmother let out a tear-choked laugh. "He is stubborn." Then her face crumpled again, and she tightened her grip on Devin. "But what if—"

"Let's not go there," Devin said. "Not yet."

Her grandmother nodded. "Okay." But she didn't let go of Devin's hand.

They'd been there for over an hour, just waiting. The room was too bright, too cold, too noisy and the distant beep of monitors was giving Devin a headache. Keri disappeared for a moment and returned with a box of tissues, pressing them into the older woman's hands.

"Thank you, sweetheart," she said, pulling a tissue out and dabbing at her eyes.

Keri nodded, giving her a reassuring smile before glancing at Devin, her eyes full of quiet concern. *Are you okay?*

Devin looked away. She wasn't.

"Mrs. Conner?" A doctor stood in the doorway. She was tall, taller than Devin, with a no-nonsense posture. Her red hair was pulled back into a ponytail, her green eyes sharp. Her voice was crisp and authoritative, the kind that expected immediate attention.

Her grandmother quickly got to her feet. Devin rose beside her, her stomach twisting.

The doctor's expression was neutral, unreadable. "Let's go somewhere quiet where we can talk in private." She held the swinging door open for them and motioned to a small room down the hall.

As they followed, the noise of the waiting room faded. No crying children, no beeping monitors. Just the rhythmic click of the doctor's shoes against the tile, and the pounding of Devin's heart in her ears.

In contrast to the chaos in the waiting room, the small consultation room was unnaturally quiet. The fluorescent lights buzzed overhead, and Devin could hear the distant murmur of voices from the nurses' station down the hall. The doctor gestured for them to sit at the small table in the center of the room.

Devin's grandmother hesitated for only a moment before sinking into a chair. Devin sat beside her, and Keri took the seat on the other side, her presence a quiet steady reassurance.

The doctor pulled up a stool, sitting across from them, her hands folded in her lap. "I'm Dr. Ross," she said, her tone professional. "I've just reviewed your husband's scans, Mrs. Conner. He has a serious concussion, but the good news is that there's no sign of a brain bleed. That said, we need to monitor him closely for the next twenty-four hours."

Devin took her grandmother's hand and closed her eyes.

Her grandmother let out a small, shaky sob, covering her mouth with her hands. "But he hasn't woken up," she whispered.

Dr. Ross nodded. "That's expected with a severe concussion. His body needs time to recover. We'll be keeping him in the ICU overnight."

Devin's grandmother gripped her hands together tightly in her lap. "And his arm?"

"It's been set, and he'll need to keep it in a cast for about six weeks," the doctor explained. "It should heal without complications."

A small relieved sound escaped from Devin's grandmother.

"When can we see him?" Devin asked, her voice steadier than she felt.

Dr. Ross glanced at the clock on the wall. "Once he's moved to a room, you'll be able to see him one at a time, but only for a few minutes every hour. Right now, we need to focus on letting him rest."

Her grandmother nodded. "Thank you, doctor."

"I'll check in again later, but in the meantime, if you have questions, let one of the nurses know."

Devin and Keri both stood, watching as the doctor left the room. The door clicked shut behind her. Her grandmother let out a long, shuddering breath and turned to Devin. "He's going to be okay?"

Devin reached for her grandmother's hand. "Yeah, Grandma. He's going to be okay."

Even as she said it, she wasn't sure who she was trying to convince more—her grandmother or herself.

CHAPTER TWENTY-TWO

Devin sat in one of the stiff plastic chairs, her arms crossed, foot tapping in an uneven rhythm against the tile floor. Her grandmother sat beside her, silent and small, hands folded in her lap, eyes closed. They'd been waiting over three hours for Devin's grandfather to be assigned a room in the ICU, and neither of them had left the waiting room other than to use the restroom.

Keri had left an hour before to get food, returning with burgers and fries, but none of them had much of an appetite. Devin unwrapped hers, took a bite, and chewed without tasting it. Her grandmother held the unopened burger in her lap, too worried to eat.

"You don't have to stay," Devin said. She knew Keri had a business to run, and a million other things she could be doing instead of sitting in this awful, fluorescent-lit limbo.

"I want to be here," Keri said, taking Devin's hand. "I have staff who can cover for me. You're stuck with me."

Devin squeezed Keri's hand. "Thank you."

An hour later, a nurse in blue scrubs appeared in the waiting room, clipboard in hand, calling out Devin's grandmother's name. The room was ready. Finally.

They followed the nurse through the halls. The ICU waiting room, compared to the one they'd just left, was much quieter, less chaotic, less frantic. For the first time in hours, Devin allowed her shoulders to relax. The nurse showed Devin's grandmother to her grandfather's room, and the two of them headed down another hallway.

Devin watched her go, her frail frame disappearing through the doorway. A part of her wanted to follow, to see her grandfather right away, but she knew this moment belonged to her grandmother. She had waited long enough.

They stood outside the room, leaning against the wall, waiting. Keri touched Devin's arm, grounding her. Devin turned to her. "Thank you for being here," she whispered.

Keri took Devin's hand in hers and raised it to her lips. "You're welcome."

When Devin's grandmother emerged a few minutes later, she looked shaken but composed, her lips pressed in a thin line. "He woke up," she said. "But he didn't say anything."

Devin nodded. That was something, at least.

It was her turn then. She stepped inside the small room, her pulse a steady drum in her ears. Her grandfather lay in the hospital bed, surrounded by wires and tubes, his skin pale against the white sheets. He looked smaller in that bed, the sheet pulled up to his shoulders. When his eyelids fluttered open and their eyes met, relief flooded through her. Before he fell asleep again, the corners of his lips lifted in a brief smile. It was almost imperceptible, but Devin saw it.

She stepped closer to the bed and touched his cheek. "I love you, Grandpa." Her voice cracked. "You have to get better. Grandma and I need you." She leaned down and lightly kissed his forehead before leaving the room.

When she stepped back into the hallway, the afternoon sun shone through the hospital windows in slanted beams. She didn't know what time it was. She was so tired she could barely stand.

Was it just this morning that she woke up in bed with Keri beside her? Keri was in the waiting room, sitting next to her grandmother.

Devin exhaled. "You're still here."

"Of course I am," Keri said, offering a small smile.

And for the first time all day, Devin let herself lean into it.

As the sky darkened, the hospital grew quiet. The waiting room had emptied some, leaving only one other family huddled in hushed conversation. Devin and Keri sat side by side, their shoulders touching. The hours dragged on. Devin and her grandmother had gone into her grandfather's room a few more times, only staying several minutes, and were back in the waiting room, waiting.

Keri stretched her legs out in front of her and glanced at Devin. "You should try to get some sleep."

Devin scoffed. "Not happening."

"I figured," Keri said, a small smile in her voice. She reached into her bag and pulled out a bottle of water. "At least drink something."

Devin twisted off the cap. The cool water helped clear the fog from her brain, but only a little. She leaned her head back against the wall and closed her eyes, listening to the distant murmurs of nurses and the steady rhythm of the hospital at night.

Sometime past midnight, Devin's grandmother stirred and sat up, rubbing her temples. Devin moved to sit beside her, wrapping an arm around her thin shoulders. "He's going to be okay," Devin whispered, though she wasn't sure if she was reassuring her grandmother or herself. Her grandmother nodded but said nothing. They sat like that for a while, the three of them—Devin, her grandmother, and Keri—waiting for the next opportunity to see her grandfather.

The waiting room was dimly lit in the early morning. The quiet hum of machines and the beeping of monitors echoed in the hallways. Devin sat curled up in a chair but hadn't slept. Her grandmother was beside her, looking as worn out as Devin. Maybe more.

She had convinced Keri to go home a little after midnight. But she was back at seven a.m., balancing a cardboard tray of coffees and a bag from Manny's.

"Good morning," Keri said, setting the food on the small table between them. She handed Devin a coffee, then one to her grandmother.

Devin kissed Keri's cheek before wrapping her hands around the coffee cup, soaking in its warmth. Her grandmother gave Keri a weary smile before taking a slow sip.

"Any change?" Keri asked, as she sank into one of the stiff plastic chairs.

Devin shook her head. "We've been in a few times. He's woken up once or twice. But only for a minute or two." Her voice was hoarse, rough from lack of sleep. She rubbed a hand over her face and yawned. "He still hasn't spoken."

Devin watched her grandmother unwrap a burrito and take a small bite. She looked pale and fragile and it worried Devin.

Keri handed her a burrito. "You need to eat," she said.

Devin peeled back the foil and took a bite. She loved Manny's breakfast burritos, but she barely tasted this one. She forced herself to take another bite and tried to think positively. Her grandfather had to be okay. "I feel so helpless. I want to do something," she said to Keri, her voice a whisper so her grandmother wouldn't hear.

Keri rested her hand on Devin's knee. "You're doing it."

Devin nodded. She hated feeling helpless and vulnerable. But Keri was right. There was nothing to do but be here, to wait, to hope. She glanced at her grandmother, noting how her eyelids drooped. It had been a long night, and she could see her exhaustion.

"Grandma, why don't you go home for a little while?" Devin said gently. "Mikey needs to be fed, and you need to get some sleep."

Her grandmother shook her head. "I don't want to leave."

Devin reached for her hand. "I know, but you need to take care of yourself too. Grandpa wouldn't want you to run yourself into the ground. Just go home for a few hours, hug Mikey, take a nap. I'll be here."

Her grandmother hesitated, glanced down the hall to her husband's room, then back at Devin. "All right. But only for a little while. You'll call me if anything changes?"

"I promise," Devin assured her.

Keri stood, already reaching for her keys. "I'll take you."

Devin's grandmother rose and cupped Devin's cheek. "I love you."

"I love you too, Grandma." She watched as Keri helped her grandmother gather her things and lead her toward the exit. Devin turned back toward her grandfather's room. She rubbed the back of her neck and hoped the doctor would come talk to her soon, but also afraid of what she might say.

She's so amazing. The way she's looking at me...I can't remember the last time I was this turned on. I cup her cheek with my hand and lean in just enough to feel the warmth of her breath against my—

"Ms. Davis..."

Her lips are so soft—

"Ms. Davis."

The voice grew more insistent, and she felt a gentle nudge to her shoulder, but the warmth of the dream tried to pull back in like a siren's song.

"Ms. Davis."

This time the nudge was more a shake, and Devin peeled open her eyes. Dr. Ross stood in front of her looking, as clichéd as it sounded, fresh as a daisy. Devin, slumped in the uncomfortable chair, eyed the doctor from head to toe. She was wearing fitted lavender scrubs, and her fiery red hair was pulled back into a perfect bun. Her sculpted cheekbones drew attention to her enigmatic green eyes. Devin smiled at the thought of the doctor on the cover of a sapphic romance.

"Ms. Davis," the doctor repeated, her arms crossed over her shapely chest.

Devin sat up straight. "Sorry." She rubbed her face with both hands. "I must have dozed off."

"Have you been here all night?"

Devin nodded and looked at the clock on the wall. It had been an hour since Keri and her grandmother had left. "I finally convinced my grandmother to go home and get some sleep, but she'll be back in a couple of hours."

"May I sit?" The doctor pointed to the empty chair next to Devin.

"Of course." Devin ran a hand through her hair. Glancing down at her wrinkled clothes, she grimaced.

The doctor sat, crossed one leg over the other, and turned to Devin. "I checked on your grandfather a little while ago. He's doing better this morning."

"Was he awake?"

The doctor nodded. "Yes, and he's talking. I'd like to keep him another twenty-four hours just to be safe, but we'll move him to a regular room."

Devin wanted to hug the doctor but refrained.

The doctor stood and turned to go, stopped and turned back. "You should go home and get some sleep too. It will be a couple of hours before he gets into a room. Call the front desk later this morning. They can tell you what room he's in."

"Okay, thanks." Devin reached for her jacket.

The doctor started to walk away then stopped and turned back. "I nearly forgot. He said to tell you he wants tacos from Manny's."

Devin laughed out loud, her tension easing. "Is that okay?"

"Sure, but not until he's been moved."

The Uber pulled away, leaving Devin standing on the front step of her father's house. She glanced at the time on her phone: nine a.m. She had texted Keri and her grandmother about what the doctor had said, and that she was heading home. Just as she unlocked the door, her phone chimed with Keri's familiar buzz.

I would have come for you, Keri's message read.

Devin chuckled to herself and texted back. *You're awake?*

I slept almost 5 hours I'm good.

Yes you are. Devin added a winking face.

Keri sent back a laughing emoji. *Your gma wants to go back to the hospital at noon I offered to drive her but she said she could drive herself. She's as stubborn as he is.* It seemed to run in the family, she thought. *Thx for everything I don't know how I can ever repay you.*

You don't need to I wanted to be there for you... and your gparents.

Devin wished Keri were there to hold her. *I need a shower and sleep.*

Call me later

Of course.

TTYL

This thing with Keri was taking on a life of its own. What was she going to do about it? What was she going to do about a lot of things in her life?

Stretching her neck from side to side didn't help relieve the stiffness. Hard plastic hospital chairs should be illegal. A yawn escaped her lips. She was sleep-deprived and weary. She headed toward the shower, hoping the scalding hot water would wash away the weight of so many things: her grandfather, the house, Bo, Keri, Tracy, and not least of all, her own future.

CHAPTER TWENTY-THREE

Devin silently watched the road through the rain-streaked windshield. The heater hummed, but it was still chilly. The chill didn't help the tightness in her shoulders. She looked over at her grandfather in the passenger seat, his right arm in a cast and tucked into a sling. Dr. Ross had been clear—five days of rest. No screens. No television. No reading. Nothing that would tax his brain.

"You comfortable, honey?" her grandmother asked from the back seat, reaching over and squeezing his shoulder.

"Yes," he said, reaching back with his uninjured arm and patting her hand. "I just want to get home. I hate hospitals."

Devin pressed her lips together. No one could hate hospitals more than she did.

The rest of the drive was quiet. Each in their own thoughts, thankful that her grandfather's fall hadn't been worse than it was. He was lucky, and they all knew it.

They pulled into the driveway thirty minutes later. "Let's get you inside, Grandpa."

She got out and hurried to the other side of the car and offered a hand. "There's no hurry."

Surprisingly, he accepted her help without a fuss. Once he was standing, he swayed slightly, and Devin reached out to steady him. She wasn't used to seeing her grandfather like this—wobbly and vulnerable.

As soon as they stepped into the house, Mikey came barreling toward them, his tiny paws skittering on the hardwood floor. He leaped around her grandfather's feet, yipping in delight. He reached down to scratch behind the dog's ears. "Someone's happy to see me."

"I'll make us some lunch," her grandmother said as she hung up her coat.

"Bedroom or living room?" Devin asked her grandfather.

He nodded to the well-worn leather recliner. Devin couldn't remember it not ever being there. "I think two days in bed is plenty, don't you?" he said slowly easing into the comfortable chair.

Devin grabbed an extra pillow from the couch and handed it to him. "Can I get you anything?"

"Would you put a record on for me?"

Her grandfather had an extensive vinyl collection. He loved the classics: Sinatra, Bobby Darin, Judy Garland. Patsy Cline was one of his all-time favorites and he boasted about the time he'd seen her sing in a bar in Nashville years ago. She remembered as a child she wasn't allowed to go near the records for fear she'd scratch one. When she turned fourteen, he finally trusted her enough to let her put one on the turntable all by herself.

"Sure," Devin said. "What's your pleasure?"

He thought for a moment. "How about some Dionne Warwick? You pick which one."

Devin chuckled at his choice. "I would never in a million years have guessed that would be who you picked."

He leaned his head back and closed his eyes. "She's one of the best, still is."

Devin grinned and began looking for Warwick's greatest hits album. "That she is, Grandpa," she said as Mikey ran in and spun in tiny circles, wanting up. Devin scooped up the pocket-sized terror and handed him to her grandfather.

Devin found the record she was looking for and slid it out of its sleeve and onto the turntable. Seconds later, the warm, soulful notes of "Say a Little Prayer for You," filled the room.

Devin glanced at her grandfather. "I could download some audiobooks onto your iPad," she offered. "Might help pass the time."

He perked up. "That's a great idea. Thank you."

"Sure," Devin said. "Any preferences?"

He took a few seconds to think about it. "Something by Jeffrey Archer. I always liked his books."

Her grandmother returned with a cup of tea in each hand. She set one on the end table next to the recliner and handed the other to Devin. "I'll be right back with sandwiches," she said, hurrying back to the kitchen.

"I hope the two of you don't go overboard. I don't need to be waited on hand and foot." He picked up the cup of tea and took a sip.

"Grandma, Grandpa said we don't have to wait on him hand and foot," Devin said, reaching for a sandwich from the tray.

"Really?" She laughed, handing her husband a sandwich and potato chips piled on a plate. "Who put him in charge?"

He looked down at the little dog in his lap. "I seem to be outnumbered here, aren't I, Mikey?" Mikey's attention, however, was focused on the sandwich Devin's grandfather was holding. He shook his head and tore a tiny piece off and held it out to Mikey, who didn't hesitate to gobble it up like he hadn't eaten in a week.

Devin wondered if she'd ever have a relationship like her grandparents had, like her parents had had. Was that something she could have with Keri? That would mean staying in Morro Harbor, and she wasn't ready to commit to that. As she took a bite of her sandwich, she felt her phone vibrate in her pocket. Keri's smiling face filled the screen.

"Hi."

"Hi yourself," Keri said, her voice cheerful. "How's he doing?"

She turned to her grandfather. "Keri wants to know how you're doing, Grandpa."

"I'm being treated like I'm king for a day. I guess I can't complain," he said, feeding Mikey another piece of his sandwich.

Keri laughed. "That's good to hear. Did you remember the fundraiser is tonight, I'll understand if you want to cancel."

"Let me talk to my grandparents and I'll call you back." Devin disconnected. "The fundraiser for the Fishermen's Fund is tonight. I told Keri I'd go with her, but I can cancel if you need me."

"Don't be ridiculous, you should go. We'll be fine," her grandmother said reassuringly.

"Of course you should go," her grandfather said in agreement.

"You're sure?"

"Of course we're sure," her grandfather said.

"Okay, then I guess I'm going."

By five o'clock the sun had appeared. Devin slipped out her front door just as Keri pulled up. Locking the door behind her, she made her way to the car and climbed into the passenger seat. Keri shot her an appreciative smile.

"You look sexy," Keri said, her eyes lingering for a moment on Devin's white slacks and navy pullover that hugged her in all the right places. She pointed at Devin, then at herself. "We match."

Devin laughed. "People will think we did it on purpose." She took in Keri's multicolored skirt and the snug navy-blue sweater, casual and elegant at the same time. She'd styled her hair into a neat bun, a few strands framed her face. It took every ounce of Devin's willpower not to reach out and tuck a stray lock behind Keri's ear. She told her racing heart to slow down.

The drive to the Veterans' Memorial Building was short. She was unsure about facing dozens of townspeople. As they pulled into the parking lot, anxiety knotted her stomach. The building itself looked almost the same as it had back then. The same brick exterior, same arched windows, and except for the fresh coat of baby-blue paint that didn't do much to mask its age, it hadn't changed. Crossing the parking lot, memories washed over her—sitting cross-legged on the floor waiting for Santa to arrive, hunting Easter eggs on the front lawn with a dozen other kids and playing hide-and-seek while their parents attended a town hall meeting.

The fundraiser had drawn a crowd. As Devin and Keri stood in line, Keri slipped her hand around Devin's arm and leaned in. "There's no need to be nervous," she whispered.

Devin's back straightened. "Who says I'm nervous?"

"Your scowl," Keri said, her tone warm.

Before Devin could respond, an older man, his face shaded by a faded green ball cap, walked up. He looked familiar, but she couldn't recall his name.

"Devin?" he said, his voice that of a lifelong smoker. "You probably don't remember me, I'm Benny Wilson, I used to work on the docks. I unloaded your dad's boat every day for years."

She reached out her hand. "Of course, Mr. Wilson. How are you?"

The man grasped her hand in a firm shake. "I can't work the docks no more. I injured my back real bad. If it hadn't been for the Fisherman's Fund helping me out for a few months till I got back on my feet, I don't know how I'd have gotten by. I have your dad to thank for that. We're all going to miss him."

Devin forced a polite smile. "I'm glad they could help you out."

He tipped the bill of his cap and walked away.

Keri took Devin's hand. "Are you okay?"

Devin nodded, but her mind reeled. She was about to say something when a woman's voice interrupted her thoughts.

"Devin, right? Patrick's daughter?" A redheaded older woman had walked up and placed a hand on her arm. "I just wanted to say I'm so sorry about your father. He was a good man. We're all going to miss him."

Devin managed to mumble, "Thank you," before the woman gave Devin's arm a gentle squeeze, and walked away.

Before she had time to think about what the woman had said, a gray-haired man stepped forward, a somber look on his face.

"I'm so sorry about your father. He helped fix my boat when I couldn't afford a mechanic. Wouldn't take a dime."

"I'm glad he could help," Devin said, before the man blended back into the crowd.

Keri squeezed Devin's hand and whispered in her ear, "How are you doing?"

"I don't know." Devin's brow furrowed. The man these people were talking about sounded like an entirely different person, someone patient, and kind...and sober. The man these people were describing wasn't the man she knew.

As they approached the front of the line, Devin's shoulders tensed. On the ticket table sat a framed photo of her father standing on the dock, a net slung over his shoulder and a grin stretched across his weathered face. The sign beside the photo read, "In Memory of Patrick Davis—A True Friend to Our Community."

The woman collecting tickets smiled warmly. "You're Devin."

Devin could only nod.

"The Fisherman's Fund has helped so many people," she said. "He won't be forgotten. That's for sure."

Like he forgot about me? Devin thought. Forcing a nod, she swallowed down the tightness in her throat. "Thank you." The woman beamed and waved them inside. The moment they were out of earshot, Devin's mask cracked. "I need a drink."

Keri didn't hesitate, steering them toward the makeshift bar set up near the back wall. Round tables draped in white cloths crowded the room. Other tables laden with silent auction items lined a side wall, and someone was setting up a microphone on the stage at the front. Food aromas permeated the air.

Devin leaned awkwardly against the bar. They'd just arrived, and she was ready to go.

"What'll it be?" the blond bartender, who looked like he'd rather be surfing, asked Keri.

"Chardonnay, please."

He looked at Devin. "And you?"

"Tequila. And a beer," Devin said, her voice strained.

He poured the wine and handed it to Keri. Then pushed a shot class of clear liquid and a lime wedge across the bar to Devin.

Without a word, she threw it back in one gulp and sucked on the lime. The tequila burned, but it was a welcome hit.

"Another?" the bartender asked.

Devin shook her head. "Just the beer."

The bartender handed her a bottle. She wrapped a paper napkin around it then took a long pull. They found a small corner to lean against the wall and sip their drinks.

"I didn't know he was so…" Devin trailed off, staring into space as if the answers floated in the ether. "Everyone keeps talking about him like he was such a great guy. I don't—I don't remember him that way. At least not after Mom died."

Keri nodded, giving Devin space to sort through her thoughts. "People are complicated," she said gently. "But I can tell you that a few years after you left, I did see a change in him. We never talked about what happened, and he never apologized, but he was pleasant whenever we ran into each other."

Devin took another sip of her beer. "If he did change, why didn't he try to contact me?"

"I can't answer that, Devin. I wish I could."

They stood there, side by side, as the room filled. Devin wasn't sure what to think or feel. All she knew was that if she stayed in Morro Harbor, the ghosts of her past wouldn't stay buried, and the thought of confronting them was unsettling.

Devin recognized many of the people but many she didn't. Her gaze landed on a familiar, reassuring face walking toward them with a smile. Frank wrapped his arms around her. "How's my favorite goddaughter?" he asked, concern etched on his face.

Devin returned the hug. "I'm your only goddaughter," she said, chuckling.

"Yes, you are." He smiled. "I'm glad you came. I think your dad would be too."

Devin wasn't so sure. "I don't know about that."

Frank's eyebrows knitted together. "He may not have ever said it to you, but he was proud of you."

Devin scowled. "It would have been nice if he'd told me that."

Frank shook his head and shrugged. "He was stubborn, and he let pride get in the way sometimes."

"Yet, he helped everyone he could but ignored his daughter. I don't know if I can ever forgive him."

Keri slipped her arm around Devin's waist. The warmth of her touch felt like a lifeline.

"I know, it doesn't make any sense." He paused and glanced around the room. "Hey, why don't you take a look at the auction items and get something to eat, and I'll find you later."

Devin nodded. "Yeah. We'll do that."

With Keri's arm still around her, they headed to the tables overloaded with donated items.

It was after eleven when they returned to Devin's. She was emotionally depleted. She'd lost track of the number of people who stopped to share a tidbit about her father. She'd pasted on a smile and thanked them, but her insides were in knots, and by the end of the night her brain was fried. "I don't think I'll be much fun to be around, but do you want to come in?"

Keri hesitated, searching her eyes. "It's been an emotional night for you," she said, cupping Devin's cheek. "I can't believe I'm saying this, but I don't think sex is the answer."

Devin leaned her head back against the seat, letting out a sigh. Turning to Keri, she whispered, "Could you just hold me?"

Keri took her hand and nodded. "I can do that."

CHAPTER TWENTY-FOUR

Devin stood in the kitchen, eyes fixed on the coffeepot, willing it to hurry and brew the magic elixir she needed to function. The night had been long, and even though Keri's arms had been wrapped around her, she hadn't slept much. Her fingers absentmindedly fingered the charm on her mother's necklace as her mind wrestled with the contradiction of her father. To her, he had been a neglectful, homophobic drunk. But to the townspeople, he was a kind, caring man who'd give someone the shirt off his back without hesitation. She didn't know what to think.

The soft shuffle of feet drew her from her thoughts. Keri entered the kitchen wearing the same colorful skirt and navy sweater from the night before. Even with her hair a tousled mess, she was beautiful.

"Morning," Keri said, a yawn stretching her words as she slipped an arm around Devin's waist and pressed a kiss to her cheek.

"Morning." Devin managed to smile. "You hungry? I can make some toast."

Keri shook her head. "I wish I could stay, but I've got to get to work before the morning deliveries show up. I don't want the UPS guy leaving cases of wine on the sidewalk."

Devin reached into the cupboard and pulled down a travel mug. "How about a cup to go?"

"That would be great." Keri leaned against the counter, watching Devin. The rich aroma filled the kitchen.

Devin snapped the lid on and handed the mug over. "Thanks for staying last night."

Keri's fingers brushed against hers, setting butterflies free in Devin's stomach.

For a moment, they stood there gazing out the window, simply enjoying each other's company.

"I'll call you later?" Keri said.

"Yeah." Devin nodded. "I'll be here."

Keri pressed another soft kiss to Devin's cheek before walking to the front door. Devin's lips curled into a smile as she watched the sway of Keri's hips, the gentle click of the door bringing her back to reality.

She topped off her coffee, cradling its warmth in her palms. Her gaze drifted out to the small, dirt backyard. The morning breeze stirred the weeds, the only touch of green other than the sycamore tree whose branches swayed in the wind. Her father had planted the tree when she was a kid, promising it would grow tall and strong, just like she would. That had been back when he was still her hero.

Devin sipped her coffee as she contemplated the day ahead. She'd hold off on a shower, she was just going to get dirty working in the garage. Taking another sip, she sighed. Time to get started. The garage wasn't going to empty itself. As she pulled on an old pair of jeans and a T-shirt, she reminded herself to ask her grandparents about a realtor. She'd meant to do that two weeks ago but kept putting it off.

Devin wiped her hands on her jeans. She'd spent the morning sorting through boxes and there was still more to go. It didn't help that her back was killing her. She glanced at her phone. It was almost noon. Frank would be there soon to look at her father's tools and fishing gear.

Devin screwed the top off a bottle of water and thought back to the previous night. The fundraiser had been draining. They'd bid on auction items, eaten dinner and made small talk with people who had known her father, and a few others from high school. She'd won a basket of cookies and muffins from the bakery, and the wine and cheese baskets Keri had donated had gone for over $200 each. But the night had been emotionally taxing.

The roar of an engine pulled her attention to the front of the house. Frank's truck pulled into the driveway next to her Jeep. He climbed out, wearing his usual easy smile. "Morning," he called. "How's it going?"

"I've been at it for almost three weeks, and I'm still not done. I thought I'd be back in the Bay Area by now."

"Why are you in such a hurry to leave?" he asked. "You know your grandparents would love it if you stayed."

Devin ran a hand through her sweat-drenched hair. "I know."

Frank let it drop. "Did you and Keri have a good time last night?"

Devin shrugged. "Honestly?"

Frank nodded.

"It was exhausting. The only thing anyone wanted to talk about was him."

"Well, the Fisherman's Fund was his baby, so it kind of was a party for him."

"Well, I didn't know that, so I was blindsided."

"Would you have gone if you'd known?"

Devin thought about it. "Probably not."

Frank smiled. "Then I'm glad you didn't know." Frank moved into the garage, running his hands over the tools on the workbench. Some of them had rusted over the years. "The salt air sure takes a toll on things."

"It does. Can they be cleaned up?"

"Yeah. It's amazing what a little naval jelly and elbow grease can do."

"Take anything you want. Hell, take 'em all."

Frank stacked the tools he wanted in a box. Devin watched from her seat on the ground. She didn't feel like talking, and Frank seemed to understand. After a few minutes, he turned to look at her. "Hey, how's your grandfather? I heard he fell off a ladder?"

"Yeah. He'll be okay. Concussion and a broken arm. He had no business on a ladder cleaning the gutters." She closed her eyes and rolled her neck, releasing the tension in her shoulders. "The doctor says he needs to take it easy for at least five days, not overdo it."

Frank shook his head. "He should have called me to do that."

Devin stood wiping sweat from her forehead. "He could have asked me too."

Frank chuckled and turned to the fishing gear piled in the corner. He picked up a fishing rod, and his expression softened. "I can't count how many times Patrick and I fished together." His eyes crinkled at the edges. "Those were good times."

"You still fish much?" she asked.

"Not as much as I'd like. But I'll put these to good use."

"I'm sure he would've liked that."

Frank loaded the first box of tools into the bed of his truck. Devin shifted from foot to foot, her arms crossed over her chest. "Do you know anyone else who might need tools?"

"I'll ask around," he said.

Devin hesitated. "What about his fishing boat?"

Frank's brow furrowed, creating wrinkles on his forehead. "You're not going to keep it?"

"I'm not staying."

"Devin, your grandparents aren't getting any younger and you're their only grandchild."

She frowned. "You don't think I know that?"

He shrugged and pretended to examine a fishing hook. Without looking at her, he said, "And there's a pretty girl who I'm sure would like you to stay."

"Frank, please just leave it alone."

"Just…think about it," he said. "Don't sell the boat right away. You might feel different in a few weeks."

She started to tell him she didn't think she'd still be here in a few weeks, but didn't have the energy, so she kept her mouth shut.

"You gonna be okay?" he asked.

"Yeah. I'll be fine."

"All right. You know you can call me if you need anything." He lifted the second box of tools into his truck, then came back for the fishing gear. "Give your grandparents my best and have them call me if I can help with anything...including the gutters." He hugged her, climbed into his truck and leaned his head out of the window. "I'm your godfather, Devin. I'm always gunna be here for you. If you let me." With a wave, he backed out of the driveway and drove off down the street.

She stood alone in the garage and let the tears fall.

CHAPTER TWENTY-FIVE

Devin continued to sort through the remaining boxes and cabinets, most of which ended up in the "to donate" or the dump pile. It was after four o'clock when she taped the last box closed. Stretching out the stiffness in her back, she surveyed the garage. Only fishing gear, surfboards, tools, and three groups of boxes remained—donations, things she'd keep, and things to go to the dump.

It was kind of sad that after whittling it all down, how little of it she'd keep. She hadn't known what to expect when she began cleaning out her father's house, but she hadn't expected the emotional journey it had taken her on.

She was filthy. Streaks of dirt covered her arms, and a fine layer of grime clung to her skin. Her hair stuck to the back of her neck, and her muscles ached from hours of physical work. She was starving. A shower came first. She headed inside, stopping in the kitchen for a cold beer on her way to the back of the house.

Before she'd unscrewed the top, her phone rang, a local number she didn't recognize. She debated letting it go to voice mail but swiped to answer.

"Hello?"

"Devin?"

She recognized the deep voice. Why was Bo calling her?

"Yeah."

There was a pause, then Bo's voice again. "I, uh, I need a ride to my meeting. I know it's last minute, but my mom's not feeling well, and dad's got a downtown thing. Wren has a class. I can't ask a friend. I haven't told anyone I'm in AA."

She didn't ask why he hadn't told his friends. She, of all people, understood the need to keep some things private.

"Okay…" She looked at the unopened beer still cold in her hand. "Where is it?"

"The Unitarian Church in SLO."

"What time?"

"Six."

"All right. I'll pick you up at five fifteen. Text me your address." She ended the call and stood there for a moment, staring at the bottle in her hand. She sighed and set it back in the fridge.

By the time she'd showered and dressed, the sun had begun to set, casting long shadows across the house. She pulled on a clean pair of jeans and her favorite San Francisco State sweatshirt, grabbed her keys and headed to the Jeep.

The address Bo had texted was at the south end of town. She pulled up in front of an aging apartment building that had seen better days and was desperately in need of a coat of paint. There was no grass, only dirt, a few weeds, and a lone dandelion.

Bo was waiting on the sidewalk, one hand shoved into the pocket of his jacket and the other still in a sling pressed against his chest. "Thanks," he mumbled as he slid into the passenger seat without looking at her.

"No problem," she said. She didn't have any plans with Keri or her grandparents. The garage was done, and the house was almost empty. But he didn't need to know any of that.

The drive was silent and uncomfortable. Bo stared out the passenger window. They passed the high school, the football field lined for the season, the bleachers empty. It brought back memories of their time in high school, the four of them: Devin,

Keri, Bo, and Melissa. If she let herself, she could hear the cheer of the crowd as Bo scored the winning touchdown in the game against Atascadero; her and Melissa's laughter at one of his stupid jokes; Bo, Melissa, and Keri standing right behind her at her mother's funeral. They had all been so close, once.

Devin swung into a parking space at the church.

"You don't have to wait. I can catch a ride back," he said, opening the door.

"I'll wait."

"Fine," he grumbled, but hesitated before getting out. "Thanks."

"I'm happy to help," she said, and she meant it. She watched him walk into the building, his shoulders still hunched. When the door closed behind him, she leaned back in her seat. The streetlights flickered on, casting a soft glow over the parking lot. She reached for her phone, brought up the Gerri Hill novel she'd been reading, and settled in to wait, her mind drifting back to the three of them, and to a time before their lives changed forever.

An hour and ten minutes later, Bo crossed the parking lot to her Jeep. He climbed in, pulling the door closed with his good arm. She pulled out of the parking lot. He was silent for the entire drive, his expression unreadable. Devin could see the tightness in his jaw and wondered what was going on in his head. He looked like he was wrestling with something. She knew better than to ask questions. She didn't want to push her luck, grateful they'd gotten to the church without Bo yelling at her. She hoped her luck would hold until they were back in Morro Harbor.

The road was empty, but Devin focused on the dark stretch of highway ahead. Deer were known for darting across this section of road, so she kept her hands steady on the wheel and didn't let her mind wander.

Thirty minutes later, she pulled up in front of his apartment building. He didn't say anything as he reached for the door handle, his movements slow and deliberate. The door opened, and just before it closed, she heard a mumbled, "Thank you."

CHAPTER TWENTY-SIX

Devin sat at the kitchen table, a steaming mug of coffee cradled between her hands, her iPad propped up against the fruit bowl as she read the local news. She'd only been up for an hour and wasn't fully awake. She muffled a yawn and took a sip of coffee.

The loud knock at the front door startled her. She grudgingly made her way through the house, the linoleum kitchen floor cold beneath her bare feet. Peeking through the small window, she groaned. Miranda...again, in uniform, her badge catching the sunlight, her hand resting on her gun belt. This wasn't a social call. Devin opened the door but didn't bother hiding her frown.

"You really know how to ruin a morning," Devin said dryly.

Miranda didn't smile. "You ready to sell the house yet?"

Devin's jaw tightened. "No, not yet."

Miranda frowned. Just a little, but enough for Devin to notice. "I need you to look at something," she said, reaching into her pocket. "The security tape from the art gallery." Miranda pulled out her phone, opening a video.

The grainy footage showed the outside of Wine Time. Streetlights cast long shadows in the early-morning darkness. A figure stepped into view. It was definitely a woman in a hooded sweatshirt, pulled over her head. There was no mistaking who it was. The woman raised a hammer and slammed it against the window. Glass exploded, scattering like sparkling confetti. The woman didn't stick around. She turned and ran, disappearing from the camera's view.

Devin's mouth dropped open.

Miranda focused her gaze on Devin. "Do you know who it is?"

"Yeah. Her name's Tracy Miller. She's my ex. I can't believe…I didn't think she'd…" Devin trailed off, staring at the frozen image of the shattered window. "I can't believe she'd do something like this."

"Were you aware she was in town?"

"She showed up a week ago," Devin said. "I have a restraining order out against her. I threatened to call the police. I assumed she went back to the Bay Area. I haven't seen her since. I had no idea she was still here."

Miranda slipped her phone back into her pocket, her expression unreadable. "You think she punctured Keri's tire?"

Devin nodded. "That would make sense."

"There's no camera in that parking lot. No witnesses, either," Miranda said. Her voice had a practiced neutrality. Devin knew it well—had used it herself once upon a time.

"Will you write up the report as a felony?" Devin asked. "Even with insurance it's going to cost Keri a grand to replace the window."

Miranda hesitated a beat. "I will. But as you know the district attorney has the final say."

They stood there, the gulf between them a mile wide, and Devin felt exposed. She wasn't wearing a bra. Her hair was a tangled mess, the neck of her T-shirt was stretched out and two sizes too big.

"I'll have my officers keep an eye out for her," Miranda said. "We'll check the local hotels."

"She doesn't have much money. I'd start with the cheapest ones."

"Okay." Miranda shifted her weight, looking uncomfortable for the first time. "Do you think your ex...I mean, is she crazy enough to hurt Keri?"

Devin opened her mouth to say no but stopped. She honestly didn't know. She would never have guessed Tracy could commit extortion, or grand theft, right under Devin's nose, but she had. Who knew what she was capable of?

"I'm not sure..." she said. "I really don't know. She's never been violent that I know about."

Miranda's expression hardened. She nodded once, turned to leave, but stopped and turned back, her eyes full of contempt. "I wish you'd never come back here. You should leave." Without another word, she strode down the path to her vehicle.

Devin closed the door and leaned her head against it. She hoped the rest of her day was better than the start of it. With an audible sigh, she pushed away and walked back to the kitchen. Her coffee was cold, the iPad screen dimmed, and outside, dark clouds obscured the sun. She reheated her coffee in the microwave. While she waited, she called Keri.

Keri answered on the second ring. "What a nice surprise."

"Hi. I wanted to give you a heads-up. Miranda might be on her way over. She's not in a good mood this morning."

Keri let out a low groan. "What now?"

Devin hesitated. The microwave beeped, but she didn't move to open it. "She asked me to look at the security footage from the art gallery. The person who broke the window...it was Tracy."

"What? Tracy, your ex? Are you sure?" Keri's voice rose. Devin pictured her standing in the middle of her living room, with one hand on her hip, eyes wide.

"Yeah, I'm sure."

"Is she's still in town?"

"I don't know. She hasn't contacted me since she showed up here, but...I think she might've been the one who punctured your tire, too."

Keri didn't say anything. All Devin could hear was the sound of her breathing on the other end.

"Keri? Are you still there?"

"Yes. Thanks for letting me know." Her voice was flat.

Devin opened the microwave, pulled her coffee out, and took a cautious sip. "I didn't want to freak you out. I just thought you should know."

"No, I'm glad you called." Keri's voice shifted, softer. "Why is she doing this?"

"I don't have a clue. She said she wants me back. Which is never going to happen," Devin rushed to add. "She might see you as a threat."

Again, Keri didn't say anything, but Devin knew the wheels were turning in her head. "Do you think she could be violent?"

Devin massaged her forehead with her free hand. "Honestly, Keri, I don't know. I wouldn't have thought she'd do half the things she's done." She paused. "She seems a little desperate. I don't think she has a place to live, or a job for that matter."

"Great," she said with a hint of sarcasm. "Just what I need, a crazy person after me." She sighed. "Do you want to get out of the house for a bit? We could drive up to Cambria or maybe go to the beach."

Devin's shoulders relaxed, a smile tugging at her lips. "Yeah. I'd like that. I've been cooped up in the garage for two days. I could use some fresh air."

"How about noon. We can get lunch somewhere?"

"Sounds perfect. I'll pick you up."

Devin disconnected and took a sip of coffee. The idea of fresh air, of the ocean breeze, seemed to chase away the chill that had settled over her since watching the video.

She sat back down at the table and tapped her iPad, but before she could return to her favorite news site, her phone chimed. It was her grandmother.

"Grandma, is something wrong?"

"No, dear. Your grandpa asked me to call you to see if you could finish cleaning the gutters. Which I told him he should have done to begin with."

Devin's heart rate returned to normal. "Of course I can. Is tomorrow okay? I'd do it today, but Keri and I have plans."

"That's fine, dear. You need to get out and have some fun." Her grandmother's voice softened, wrapping Devin in warmth. "How was the fundraiser?"

Devin cradled her coffee mug. "It was fine. They had a good turnout." She hesitated, then added, "More than a few people came up to me. Told me how much they'd miss Dad."

Her grandmother hummed thoughtfully. "I'm sure they did. Patrick helped a lot of people." There was a pause. "I hope it wasn't too hard on you."

"It was okay." Devin's voice wavered, and she took a steadying sip of coffee, forcing a smile even though her grandmother couldn't see it.

"All right, I won't keep you. You have a good time with Keri today. Go enjoy yourself."

"I will. I'll see you tomorrow, okay?"

"Okay, dear. Love you."

"Love you too." Devin ended the call and let herself breathe. In and out.

Devin pulled her Jeep into a space in front of the wine bar, its large front window covered with plywood. She turned off the engine and sat for a moment, fingers still curled around the steering wheel. The street was quiet. A gentle breeze stirred the leaves on nearby trees. Her eyes drifted to the sidewalk where Keri waited, shifting her weight from one foot to the other. Dressed in tight skinny jeans and a faded green sweatshirt, she'd pulled her hair into a ponytail. Strands had escaped and danced around her face. She looked beautiful.

When Keri spotted her, a smile lit up her face and she hurried over and slipped into the passenger seat. "Hey, you," Keri said, closing the door behind her.

"Hey." Devin let the warmth of Keri's presence settle around her. "I was thinking Manny's Tacos."

Keri's eyes lit up. "You know I'll never say no to Manny's. Let's do it."

They drove with the windows down, their conversation light. Tourists with sunburned faces, carrying cheap souvenirs, strolled down Main Street, and locals hurried about their business.

They ordered at the counter and took their tacos to a weathered picnic table beneath a faded green awning. The smell of grilled carne asada and cilantro filled the air. They ate in silence, the only sounds the crunch of tortilla chips and the low buzz of conversation from the other tables.

Devin could feel Keri's eyes on her.

"Do you think she's still in town?" Keri finally asked.

Devin picked at the edge of her taco. "Tracy?"

Keri frowned. "Yes, Tracy."

"I don't know…maybe?" Devin raised her eyes to meet Keri's. "She hasn't contacted me since the day you saw her at my place."

Keri's expression tightened. "Should I be worried?"

Devin reached out and squeezed Keri's hand. "I wish I could say no…but I really don't know."

Keri's eyes widened. "How was she ever hired by the police department?"

Devin shook her head, her taco forgotten. "I asked myself that every day. We had to undergo a psychological evaluation and a lie-detector test. I don't know how she passed either of them."

"A sociopath could," Keri said.

Devin nodded.

They finished lunch and walked back to the Jeep. "How about we drive out to Montana De Oro?" Devin suggested.

"Sure, sounds good to me."

The Jeep hugged the curves of the winding road to the state beach. Cliffs dropped away from the rocky landscape, revealing the ocean crashing below. In the distance, a thin layer of fog blurred the horizon.

Montana De Oro Beach was rocky, the small stones worn smooth from continuous tumbling in the surf. Waves crashed against jagged formations, the water a deep, churning blue. In the distance, Morro Rock jutted out of the water against a brilliant blue sky.

They walked along the shore, not talking, their fingers laced together, the ocean a steady roar in the background. The air was cool and damp. Devin let it wash over her. At the far end of the beach, they stopped to watch the waves rush in, then roll back out.

Keri broke the silence. "Are you almost done with the house?"

"Almost. Just the kitchen left. It's mostly junk. I should find a realtor and get it on the market soon."

Keri didn't respond. When Devin turned to look at her, catching the way her lips pressed together, her eyes focused on the waves. Devin's stomach tightened. "I've been honest with you from the beginning," Devin said softly.

Keri's face gave her away, the truth written in the downturn of her mouth. "I know. I just hoped…"

"Keri, I'm not sure I belong here."

Keri stopped walking and turned to face Devin. "But maybe you do."

The surf crashed against the rocks, the spray a fine mist on their faces. Devin stared at the horizon, the line between sky and sea a blur. She didn't know what to say. She looked down at their joined hands, at the way Keri's thumb brushed over her knuckles. "I don't know what I'm doing," Devin said. "Or where I belong."

Keri reached out and cupped Devin's cheek. "You don't have to know. But you don't have to run, either."

Devin wanted to believe that, to imagine a future that wasn't haunted by her past. She let Keri pull her closer, felt the warmth of her arms around her. Devin inhaled the salty air and let herself lean into Keri, just enough to feel anchored. The past loosened its grip, and she let herself enjoy the moment.

CHAPTER TWENTY-SEVEN

The morning fog hung heavily in the air, wrapping the town in a gray blanket. Devin pulled on her high school hoodie, the worn fabric soft against her skin. A quick breakfast of scrambled eggs, toast, and coffee fueled her trip to clean her grandparents' gutters. Driving through the thick mist felt eerie. Streets and buildings blurred at the edges, their familiar shapes muted by the fog. Everything felt shrouded in mystery.

She pulled into her grandparents' driveway. The front porch light was still on, a warm, yellow glow in the gloom. She caught her reflection in the side mirror of the Jeep. Her hair looked like she hadn't combed it that morning, and there were dark circles under her eyes. She hadn't slept well, tossing and turning all night. Her dreams had been full of Tracy's unpredictable presence and worry over Keri's safety. Every time she drifted off, a fresh wave of dread filled her, waking her once more.

Before she reached the porch, a small blur of fur came barreling around the corner of the house. Mikey ran toward her, his tiny paws skittering across the cement path, his tail wagging so fast, he almost knocked himself over.

"Hey, buddy." Devin knelt and picked him up. His warm little tongue darting out to lick her chin made her chuckle. "I'm happy to see you too."

Her grandmother opened the screen door before Devin could reach for it. "Well good morning," she said, her smile warm and welcoming. "Come in, come in. It's cold out there."

Devin stepped across the threshold and set Mikey down. The smell of cinnamon filled the air, and she wondered what goodies her grandmother had made. Her grandfather sat at the kitchen table, a blanket draped over his legs, his right arm resting in a sling. He looked pale, but his smile was as bright as ever. With a loud yip, Mikey jumped up onto his lap, curling into a tiny, warm ball.

"Hey, Grandpa." Devin bent down to hug him, and he embraced her with his good arm. "How're you doing?"

"Better every day," he said. "Your grandma's been keeping me in line."

"Good." Devin said, sitting down at the table. "You're supposed to be taking it easy."

Her grandmother set a fresh cup of coffee in front of her and then disappeared back into the kitchen, returning with a plate of warm cinnamon rolls, and even though she was full, she reached for one.

"He is. Mostly." Her grandmother shot him a look that was only half teasing. "He wanted to drive me to the store yesterday. As if I'd let him behind the wheel when he's still recovering."

He raised his good hand, a smirk pulling at his lips. "She did let me go along for the ride."

Devin took a sip of coffee and asked, "How are the audiobooks?"

"Good," Grandpa said. "That Jeffery Archer sure knows how to spin a tale."

"Yes, he does," Devin said, taking a bite of her cinnamon roll.

"How's the packing going?" her grandmother asked.

"Almost done. Just the kitchen. And I'll need to find a place to donate the last of the furniture."

"You talk to a realtor yet?" her grandfather asked.

"Not yet." Devin wiped her mouth with a napkin.

He watched her for a moment. "Are you having second thoughts about selling the house?"

She opened her mouth, not sure what to say, but her phone buzzed in her pocket. She fished it out, the screen lighting up with an unfamiliar number, but the area code was from the Haywood area. Her stomach dipped. "Hang on. I should take this." She slipped out the back door, the cold air biting against her face, and she pulled the hood of her sweatshirt over her head. "Hello?"

"Devin Davis?" The voice was crisp, professional. "This is Janeen from HR at the Haywood Police Department."

Her pulse quickened. "Yeah, hi."

"Devin, we received the reports from your psychiatrist and physical therapist. You've been cleared to return to work on light duty."

Light duty. Meaning office work, not patrol. Her grip on the phone tightened. "How much time do I have to decide?"

"We'd need to know by Monday," Janeen said. "If you decide not to come back, we'll start processing your resignation."

"All right. Thanks."

The fog curled around her, and she wrapped her arms around her waist to warm herself. Four days. She had four days to figure out what the hell she was going to do. Four days to figure out if there was anything to go back to in Haywood.

Back inside, her grandparents' faces were a mix of curiosity and concern. She pasted on a smile.

"Everything okay?" her grandfather asked.

Devin pulled her chair back up to the table. "It was work. I'm cleared to go back." She frowned. "On light duty."

Her grandmother placed her hand on Devin's and squeezed. "Is that good news?"

"I'd be behind a desk, not out on the streets," Devin said, her tone flat. "I have until Monday to decide."

Her grandparents' eyes met. Devin wished she could read minds, wished they could tell her what to do. But the decision was hers, and the weight of it was heavier than any box she'd carried out of her father's house. Did she want to return to a department where so many officers had abandoned her? Would she even be safe going back there? But if not Haywood, then where? Was the phone call a sign that she should stay where she was? Or should she move on to someplace else?

By midafternoon Devin had finished cleaning the gutters. The fog had lifted several hours ago, the sky was cloudless and there was barely a breeze. A perfect afternoon to kayak. She borrowed her grandfather's and loaded it onto her Jeep. Her grandmother handed her a bottle of water and a container of sunscreen. She gave them both a hug and promised to check in later.

She pulled into the marina, her tires crunching over gravel as she backed up to the boat launch. She was the only one there. Feeling no need to hurry, she sat for a moment, letting the peaceful afternoon settle around her. The tide was still, the water as smooth as glass—the conditions couldn't be better.

She got out, stretched until her back popped, and pulled off her hoodie, revealing a faded gray T-shirt, a relic from a soccer team she'd played on years ago. She ditched her sneakers, rolled her jeans up as high as they'd go, and tugged a battered Giants cap low over her eyes. After a quick slather of sunscreen, she pulled the kayak down, loaded her paddle, life jacket and water bottle into it, and parked the Jeep. She returned to the kayak and eased it into the water. The cold lapped at her bare feet, sending a shiver up her spine. Climbing in, she paddled the boat forward, slicing through the stillness, her worries fading.

She headed to the south end of the estuary, and settled into an easy rhythm, each stroke of the paddle cutting a smooth arc, her breathing synced. Her left arm, strained from cleaning the gutters, throbbed with each stroke, but she powered through, welcoming the burn, and forced her focus inward.

She watched the seagulls wheel overhead in lazy circles, their cries mingling with the softer calls of pelicans dipping into the water. She envied their freedom. The harbor unfolded around her—the old docks, a few derelict fishing boats mixed among sleek sailboats, and a couple of small yachts. A raft of otters lounged on the far side. Some floated on their backs, paws resting on their bellies, others held paws to keep from drifting apart. Enjoying the solitude, she watched them before paddling away. Her arm ached, and her breath didn't quite fill her lungs the way it had before the shooting. The injury had left its mark, a constant reminder of the betrayal and trauma she'd suffered but lived through.

An hour sped by, the sun climbing higher, its warmth prickling the back of her neck where the sunscreen hadn't reached. Sweat dampened the brim of her cap, her arms ached, her breath was ragged, but it felt good. So good... She stopped paddling and let the kayak drift, and the stillness engulfed her. Her heart rate and breathing slowed, and a sense of peace filled her. She enjoyed the quiet for a few minutes before she reversed course and slowly paddled back to the marina.

At the dock, she hauled the kayak out of the water and loaded it onto the Jeep. The weight challenged her tired limbs, but the physical activity had been just what she needed. As she slid her aching body into the driver's seat, her phone rang, startling her. She fumbled it out of the cupholder and looked at the screen.

Wren.

"Hi," she said.

"Hi. Are you busy?" Wren asked.

"Just finished kayaking and was heading home." She took another swig from the water bottle. "What's up?"

There was a pause. "I need a favor."

"Okay. What kind of favor?"

"My boss called me in, and I'm supposed to take Bo to his meeting tonight. Mom and Dad are both tied up. Could you take him?"

Devin hesitated. She didn't have plans, so there really wasn't a reason she couldn't, and it had gone okay the last time. At least she thought it had.

"Sure. What time?"

"Six. Same place as Monday night."

"Got it."

"I owe you, Devin."

"I love tacos."

Wren laughed. "Done."

Devin sat for a moment, wondering if Bo would be okay with it. He didn't really have a choice. She pulled out of the lot and headed home. She had just enough time to shower and grab a bite before picking him up.

The sun sat on the horizon. A palette of amber and rose painted the sky as Devin pulled up in front of Bo's apartment. He stood on the cracked concrete walkway, his expression stony.

He approached with a slight limp, his arm in a cast but no longer in a sling. Without a word, he yanked the door open. "What are you doing here?" His voice was rough.

"Wren got called into work." Devin kept her tone even. "She asked me to drive you."

Bo let out a huff. He glanced down the empty street, jaw tight, before finally climbing in. He didn't look at her as he slammed the door closed.

Devin eased away from the curb. The silence between them was tense. Bo stared straight ahead, and she didn't push.

The drive to the church was silent, the only sounds were the tires on pavement and the hum of the engine. Devin kept her eyes forward and focused on the road. The sky darkened as the sun sank behind them.

When she pulled into the small lot behind the church, Bo was already reaching for the handle. His feet crunched against the gravel. Before closing the door, he hesitated. "Thank you," he said so quietly Devin wasn't sure she'd heard it.

Then he was gone, walking up the path toward the church, his shoulders hunched with a weight only he could lift. She watched him until he disappeared through the door, and she turned back to gaze out the front window. Had she really heard him say "thank you"?

She reached for her phone on the center console. The screen lit up with the book she'd been reading, and she let its words pull her in. She didn't get far before the phone rang; the book shrinking into the corner of the screen as Keri's name appeared. "Hi," Devin said.

"Hi yourself." Keri's voice was warm. "What are you up to?"

"I just dropped Bo off at his meeting. Wren called me in for backup."

"Oh, how'd that go?" Keri chuckled quietly.

"He wasn't thrilled, but he got in. I'll call it a win."

"I would too."

"What about you? How's things at work?"

"I worked on inventory all day," Keri said, a sigh threading through the line. "But the good news is the window is getting installed tomorrow. No more plywood and duct tape."

"That's great."

"Yeah, it's been really dark in here all boarded up. I was thinking," Keri continued, "about having Chris and Bill over for dinner tomorrow. Figured I'd check if you were free?"

"I'm free."

"Good."

"I'll bring dessert."

"It's a plan."

They lingered for a moment in a comfortable silence. Then Keri let out a small laugh. "All right, I should get back to this mountain of paperwork. I'll see you tomorrow?"

"Yes, you will." When the call ended, the screen bounced back to Devin's book. Its soft glow settled against the dark interior of the Jeep.

An hour later, the passenger door opened, making Devin jump. Bo slid back into the passenger seat, his movements deliberate, his silence heavy. Devin put her phone away, turned the key. The rumble of the engine filling the space between them.

"Did the meeting go okay?" she asked, knowing she risked provoking his wrath.

"Fine."

She didn't push, just eased the Jeep out of the parking lot and headed back to Morro Harbor. Bo remained silent beside her, his gaze fixed somewhere far away, his face a stony mask. When they pulled up in front of his apartment, Bo didn't move. Devin shifted into park, her hand resting on the gearshift as she turned to look at him. "Are you okay?"

He didn't look at her. His fingers on his uninjured hand squeezed into a fist, knuckles white in the dim light. "I don't hate you."

Her thoughts spun. "I don't understand."

He swallowed. "I don't hate you." His Adam's apple bobbed up and down. "I hate myself."

She didn't say anything, unsure where this was going.

"I blamed you because it was easier than blaming myself." His voice was raw.

"Why did you blame yourself? You weren't even there."

Bo shook his head, his chin falling to his chest. "I was supposed to be. If I had been, maybe it wouldn't have happened."

"You couldn't have made Melissa come back in. She was determined to get one more run."

"Maybe I could have." His voice cracked, and a tear slid down his face. "She was my twin. Maybe she would have listened to me. Or maybe I could have gotten to her sooner than you did, pulled her out of the water faster than you did."

Devin didn't move, didn't reach out to him. She knew the fragility of this moment.

"But all I cared about was getting laid," he said, his voice a whisper. "I was fucking Kim while my sister was dying."

"Bo, we were barely eighteen," Devin said, gentle but firm. "We were kids. You made the same choice any horny teenage boy would have."

Bo shook his head. "No. I should have been there. She needed me, and I wasn't there." He did his best to stifle a sob.

Devin's hand twitched, almost reaching for him, but she stopped herself, her fingers curling against the edge of the seat.

"I'll never forgive myself," he said.

"Bo, it was an accident. There's nothing to forgive."

Bo turned to face her, his face wet with tears. "But you blamed yourself, didn't you? That's why you left. That's why you never came back."

Devin nodded. "I've lived with the guilt for the past ten years. I'm still grieving. I miss her so much." Tears began to fall down her face.

When Bo spoke again, his voice was filled with anger. "You left me here. Alone. I had to deal with her loss and my guilt alone."

Her chest tightened. "You hated me. You made sure I knew it. Your anger was...I was afraid of you."

His anger dissolved as he wiped his face with the sleeve of his jacket. "I was an asshole. I am an asshole. I'm sorry. I'm so sorry."

Tears continued to slip down Devin's cheeks, but her voice held. "I think it's time you forgave yourself."

"What about you? Are you going to forgive yourself?"

She stared out the front window. Silence stretched between them.

"Devin?"

She turned to look at him. "I can try." She felt the weight she carried ease just a little bit.

They sat in silence for a moment. "My mom wants me to see a therapist," he said.

"That might be a good idea." She took a breath and let it out. "For both of us."

He wiped his face again and sat up straight. "I should go," he said, opening the door. "Thanks for the ride."

Before he could slip away, Devin reached out, her hand brushing his arm. His gaze met hers, a question in his eyes. "How about I drive you every Wednesday?"

His lips pressed together. "Does that mean you're not leaving?"

She exhaled. "I don't know. Maybe."

Bo nodded, and he climbed out of the Jeep. Devin watched him go, his steps slowed by the limp, until he disappeared around the corner of the building.

CHAPTER TWENTY-EIGHT

The sun hung low in the sky, smearing the horizon with streaks of fiery orange and pale red. The air was still, barely enough of a breeze to ruffle the leaves in the trees lining Main Street. Devin drove down the quiet street, her fingers tapping absently against the steering wheel. One of her grandfather's chocolate cream pies sat nestled in a cardboard box on the passenger seat.

Devin pulled into a parking spot in front of the vacant storefront between the wine bar and the bookstore. She sat for a moment looking at the new window, its etched glass sending back fractured bits of sunlight. She slid out of the car and stood on the sidewalk, pie in hand, staring through the grimy window of the empty shop. What kind of place would fit in with the vibe of the neighborhood? Something that would draw tourists in but also appeal to locals.

She glanced up and down the street. Was Tracy still lurking around Morro Harbor, looking for another way to get back at her? She tightened her grip on the pie box and headed to the stairs to Keri's apartment.

Before she took the first step, Chris and Bill walked out of the bookstore. "Perfect timing," Bill said, grinning and holding up a bottle of wine. "We're ready if you are." As they climbed the stairs Devin could smell something spicy drifting through the open window.

At her knock, the door opened. "Hey, come in." Keri gave them each a warm hug and placed a kiss on Devin's cheek. Keri took the pie from Devin, and their fingers brushed causing a jolt of electricity to shoot to Devin's center.

"I made chicken enchiladas," Keri said, tucking a strand of hair behind her ear. "With rice and black beans."

"Smells amazing," Chris said, already reaching for the wineglass Keri offered.

They moved into the living room, sinking into the soft cushions, glasses of wine in hand. Keri sat close to Devin, their thighs brushing. Devin breathed in Keri's scent.

"We've got a book signing on Saturday," Bill said. "It's Sapphic author Jen Lyon."

"I love her books!" Keri said. She turned to Devin. "Want to go?"

Devin nodded. "Absolutely."

The kitchen timer dinged, and Keri jumped up. "Dinner's ready."

Over plates of enchiladas, the conversation flowed easily, and Devin relaxed, almost forgetting the weight of the past few weeks. "The HR department called," she said, taking a sip of wine. "They cleared me to go back to work. Behind a desk. Not patrol."

Keri's fork paused midair. "And?"

"I need to give them an answer by Monday."

Chris and Bill shared a glance. Keri's hand settled on Devin's knee. "Is it safe to go back? I mean, considering what happened?"

Chris's eyebrows scrunched together. "What do you mean, 'is it safe'?"

Devin looked at Keri and shrugged. She set her wineglass down. "I mentioned I'd been injured, but that's not the whole story." She proceeded to tell them everything of the betrayal, leaving nothing out, including that it was Tracy who smashed the window and probably punctured Keri's tire. When she finished, the room was quiet. Chris looked stricken. Bill's hands wrapped tightly around his wineglass. Keri's fingers never left Devin's knee.

"I wouldn't go back," Chris said. "Fuck them." He lifted his wineglass and chugged down what remained.

Keri stood. "How about dessert?"

The pie was a perfect distraction, and the conversation turned to lighter things. Devin asked if anyone knew anything about the empty storefront. No one did, and they all agreed it was a shame for the space to sit empty. Devin felt a pang of something she couldn't quite name.

When they finished the last of the wine, Chris and Bill said their goodbyes, leaving Devin and Keri alone on the couch. The wine had loosened something in Devin. "I don't know what to do," Devin said, staring off into space.

"You mean to stay or go?"

Devin nodded.

Keri shifted and cupped Devin's cheek. "I hope you stay."

Devin looked at her, the softness in Keri's expression unraveling something deep inside. "On the way home from Bo's meeting last night he told me he doesn't hate me."

Keri's eyebrows raised. "Wow. That's huge."

Devin nodded and leaned into Keri's touch. "He said blaming me was easier than blaming himself."

"He blames himself for Melissa's death? Why?"

She kissed Keri's fingers. "He was going to go surfing with us, but he ditched us to get laid."

"And he thinks if he'd been there, he could have stopped Melissa from going out one more time?"

"Or he'd could have saved her."

"That's quite a burden to bear all these years. But it's no excuse for treating you the way he has."

"His parents have made it clear they don't blame me either. At Bo's court hearing they welcomed me with open arms."

"No one blames you, Devin. You need to stop blaming yourself."

"Bo said the same thing."

"Don't you think it's time you did?"

"I can try."

"That's a start," Keri said, as she leaned in and placed her lips on Devin's.

Devin closed her eyes and returned the kiss. Maybe Keri was right. Maybe it was time.

CHAPTER TWENTY-NINE

Friday morning, the fog was thick as Devin parked in front of Ms. Bell's house. The sun might come out later, but right now, it was cold.

She'd called ahead to make sure Ms. Bell was home. What Ms. Bell said about opening a bed-and-breakfast had been on her mind ever since she and Keri stopped by two weeks ago. She raised her hand to knock, but the door opened, and Ms. Bell greeted her with a hug.

"Come in, dear. I just put the kettle on."

Devin stepped inside. The air smelled of vanilla and cinnamon, and she wondered what Ms. Bell was baking. "I hope I'm not interrupting anything," Devin said, shrugging off her jacket.

"No. I just finished baking some cookies. The knitting group at the senior center loves my snickerdoodles."

They went to the living room and Devin sank onto the couch while Ms. Bell disappeared into the kitchen, returning with a tray of tea and cookies. "I'm sure they won't mind if you have a few."

Ms. Bell set the tray down on the coffee table and handed Devin a mug before taking a seat across from her.

Devin reached for a cookie, took a bite, and let a small moan escape her lips. "This is the best snickerdoodle I think I've ever had. Don't tell my grandma I said that." She winked.

"It'll be our secret." Ms. Bell chuckled. "But nobody can beat your grandfather's pies."

Devin nodded. "That's true. They are the best."

They chatted about the weather for a bit before Devin got to the point. Leaning forward, she rested her elbows on her knees and interlaced her fingers. "Do you still want to open a bed-and-breakfast for writers?"

Ms. Bell's eyes lit up. "Oh, yes. I think it's a perfect place for one, overlooking to harbor as it does. It's very inspirational."

Devin grinned. "I agree. That's why I wanted to talk to you. I have a proposition."

Ms. Bell raised an eyebrow. "Oh?"

"I like to be your partner." She gave Ms. Bell a second to take that in. "I'd use part of the money my parents left me. It's…a lot."

Lines creased Ms. Bell's forehead. "I'm sorry, I don't understand."

"My mother had a life insurance policy. My dad never touched it. He put it into a high interest savings account, with my name on it."

"No, not about that. That's none of my business." She shook her head. "You want to be my business partner?"

"Yes." Devin nodded. "We could use my capital to get it up and going." Devin tried to read the expression on Ms. Bell's face. She couldn't tell what she thought of the idea.

"Devin, bed-and-breakfasts don't make a lot of money. To be honest, most of them don't stay open long."

"I know. I did some research. And I'm okay with the risk." She gave Ms. Bell a mischievous grin. "There's just one catch."

Ms. Bell sat up a little straighter. "A catch?"

Devin took a sip of her tea before answering. "That we name it for Melissa. She dreamed about being a writer."

Ms. Bell was quiet for a moment. "I know she did. She was quite talented. It would be a wonderful way to honor her."

Devin looked out the window. The sun was doing its best to break through the fog over the ocean. She turned back to Ms. Bell. "I found a binder full of her poems while cleaning out the garage. She gave them to me a little while before the accident. I'm going to give them to her parents."

"I'm sure they'll treasure them."

"Would you read them? If you believe they're good, maybe I could get them published for her. If her family agrees.

"That's a lovely idea, and I'd be honored to read them."

Devin smiled and leaned back against the cushions. "So, what do you think about me becoming your business partner?"

Ms. Bell picked up her tea. "To be honest, I don't know what to think. I'm not saying yes, or no. There's a lot to discuss. But, if you're serious, I think we should sit down with a lawyer, so we understand what all is involved."

"Yes. You're right, we should absolutely do that."

"Okay, I'll do some research on attorneys that do that kind of work."

"Great." Devin smiled, picked up another cookie, and took a bite. "The police department in Haywood called me. I'm cleared to go back to work. I need to let them know by Monday what I'm going to do."

Ms. Bell tilted her head. "And?"

"And I'm starting to believe I could stay here," Devin said quietly.

Ms. Bell smiled. "Of course you can. Morro Harbor is your home."

"I haven't told Keri or my grandparents I'm thinking about staying. I don't want to get their hopes up."

Ms. Bell set her tea back down and looked Devin in the eyes. "Those are the people your decision will affect the most. You should talk to them."

Devin nodded. She only had the weekend to decide her future. And Ms. Bell was right. Whatever she decided would affect Keri and her grandparents almost as much as it would her.

CHAPTER THIRTY

Devin woke to a foggy Saturday morning. The mist was thick and everything outside was wet. Inside, the house was nearly empty. She'd spent Friday afternoon packing up the last of the kitchen, leaving only the coffee pot, a few appliances, and other essentials. It wasn't like she was cooking any actual meals, anyway.

The floor was cold against her feet as she padded into the kitchen. The counter was bare except for the coffee maker, a couple of mugs, and a half-empty bag of grounds. She didn't bother measuring, just dumped enough in to make it strong. The aroma filled the air, helping jump-start her brain. While the coffee brewed, she leaned against the counter, watching the gray fog swirl outside the window.

Yesterday, a handful of people had stopped by—Frank's friends and a couple of her father's fishing buddies—to sift through what was left of the tools and fishing gear. Most of it was gone now. The few leftover things were in the pile destined for the dump.

A truck from the charity shop would be there in an hour to take the remaining furniture and boxes. When they left she'd use her dad's pickup to make a run to the dump, then head to her grandparents' house. She'd stay with them until she decided what she was going to do. She had forty-eight hours to make up her mind.

After talking to Ms. Bell, a plan had started to form. It was still taking shape. And Melissa's poetry... She could edit it, put it together the way Melissa would've wanted. Publish it, maybe.

And then there was Keri. Her smile still hit her the same way it had in high school, leaving her feeling off balance. Just the thought of her stirred something in her. Their time together during the past few weeks had been amazing. The nights even better. The heat between them was undeniable, electric and consuming. Long after they'd parted, Keri's touch remained on her skin. She couldn't stop replaying the way Keri's mouth felt on hers, or the way their bodies fit together perfectly. The thought of leaving Keri again ripped at her heart. It was possible, likely even, that she was in love with her. She didn't want to walk away from that. Not again.

And Frank was right. Her grandparents weren't getting any younger. She liked the thought of being close by, helping when they needed it. They wouldn't ask for it, but that didn't mean they didn't need it. After all they'd done for her, she owed them. The more she thought about it, the more staying in Morro Harbor felt like the right thing to do.

Staring out the window, her mind drifted to the empty storefront on Main Street. She'd passed it yesterday, the big window papered over, a faded "For Lease" sign still taped to it. It tugged at something in her. She imagined kayaks and paddleboards lining one wall, surfboards hanging like art from the ceiling, and wetsuits on a rack in the back. It called to her, but did she want to be a business owner? It wasn't something she'd ever considered.

The sound of a truck engine interrupted her musing, and she blinked. It was probably the charity-shop people, early. She didn't mind. The sooner the house was empty, the sooner she could move forward.

She glanced around the kitchen. Faded wallpaper and scuffed linoleum hinted at the house's age. A dent in the wall marked

where her fifteen-year-old self had run through the house with
her surfboard. Why hadn't her father ever repaired it? Thousands
of memories surrounded her, all tangled up with grief and guilt.
Maybe if she stayed, she could make peace with them. She exhaled
slowly, pulled on sneakers and a hoodie, and walked out the front
door.

By the time Devin pulled into her grandparents' driveway, the
sun was high overhead, burning off the last of the morning fog.
Her arms ached from hauling the last of her dad's things to the
dump, and she could feel the dirt and sweat clinging to her skin. A
shower was calling her name.

Before she even had the Jeep's door open, all four pounds of
Mikey came barreling at her, his tail wagging so hard he turned
himself in a circle. Devin stepped out and picked him up with one
hand and grabbed her duffel with the other.

"Okay, okay, I missed you too!" She laughed, letting the tiny
dog lick her face.

The screen door banged open before she made it to the steps.
"Devin! I was starting to think you'd gotten lost at the dump."
Her grandmother took a step toward her, then retreated. "You
need a shower."

Her grandfather pushed open the screen door with his good
arm and stepped onto the porch. "Devin," he said, taking her in
from head to toe. "You look like hell."

"I feel like it too," Devin admitted, setting Mikey on the
ground. "How's the arm?" she asked, nodding to the sling.

"Healing up. And the concussion's better. Doctor said I'm
okay to drive."

"Thank God for that," her grandmother said. "He's been
driving me crazy, following me around like a lost puppy."

"Don't listen to her," he said with a wink. "She loves having
me around."

"Go take a shower, honey," her grandmother said, patting her
arm. "I'll have lunch ready when you get out."

Hot water streamed over her aching shoulders, washing away
the sweat and grime. If there was a heaven, this must be what it

felt like. By the time she toweled off and threw on clean clothes, she felt almost human again. Her grandparents were waiting at the kitchen table, plates of sandwiches and coleslaw in front of them. Devin slid into the empty chair just as her stomach growled.

"How's the house?" her grandfather asked after a few bites.

Devin hesitated, setting her sandwich down. "Except for a few things I'm keeping, it's empty. The truck from Achievement House Charity picked up the furniture and the rest of the boxes this morning."

Her grandfather nodded. "Did you find a realtor yet?"

She took a sip of water. "I'm thinking about staying."

Both grandparents looked up, surprised. Her grandmother tilted her head, studying her.

"Staying?" her grandfather repeated. "For good?"

"Maybe." She took a breath and explained what had transpired between Bo and her. "I think we might be able to be friends again. He's going to start seeing a therapist." She paused. "I think I might too."

Her grandfather nodded and smiled across the table at her grandmother.

"I talked to Ms. Bell the other day. She's going to turn her mother's house into a bed-and-breakfast for writers." She paused and took a sip of water before she continued, "I'm thinking about using some of the money Mom and Dad left me to partner with her. If we do, we'll name it for Melissa."

Her grandmother's eyes softened. "What a wonderful way to honor her memory."

"And there's Keri…"

Her grandmother's expression didn't change. "Keri?"

Devin felt her cheeks heat. "I'd like to see where it goes."

Her grandmother reached across the table and squeezed Devin's hand. "That's a good reason to stay too."

"I still have until Monday to decide," Devin added. "But…the thought of staying feels better than it did a few weeks ago."

Her grandfather's eyes sparkled. "Of course, we hope you stay. But whatever you decide, we're proud of you. You've been through more than most people could handle."

Devin wasn't one hundred percent sure yet, but almost.

CHAPTER THIRTY-ONE

The evening air felt warm against Devin's bare arms. A slight breeze carried the familiar briny sent of the ocean. That morning, she'd needed a sweatshirt to ward off the chill, but tonight it was pleasantly warm. Before starting up the stairs to Keri's apartment, she glanced out at the harbor. The setting sun painted a canvas of pinks and oranges behind the eclectic mix of sailboats that bobbed in the water.

The wooden stairs to Keri's apartment groaned beneath her feet, and her heart beat a little faster, not from exertion, but anticipation. When she knocked, the door opened almost at once. The sight that greeted her caused her heart to race even more. Keri's hair fell loosely around her shoulders, a few strands catching in the light. The smile she gave Devin was inviting and the glint in her eyes mischievous. Devin leaned in and placed a soft kiss on Keri's lips.

"Hi," she said softly. "Ready?"

Keri nodded and locked the door behind her. At the foot of the stairs, they turned to walk to the bookstore. Devin stopped in front of the empty storefront and peeked through a hole in the brown paper that covered the windows. She almost said something, but the words stuck in her throat. She wasn't quite ready to talk to Keri about the possibility of staying in Morro Harbor. The last thing she wanted to do was give her false hope.

Keri noticed and stopped. She looked at Devin, her brow furrowed. "What is it?"

"Nothing," Devin said, shaking her head. "Just…thinking."

Devin took her hand, and they kept walking. The bookstore was ahead, the rainbow flag that hung out front swayed in the breeze. The light from inside spilled onto the sidewalk, welcoming them. A familiar figure appeared from the other direction.

Ms. Bell smiled when she saw them, her eyes crinkling at the corners. "Well, look at this. The two of you out on the town together."

Keri chuckled. "Just the bookstore. Nothing too wild."

"Wild enough for me." Ms. Bell chuckled, then nodded at the door. "Shall we?"

Devin held the door open, and the little brass bell chimed. As Ms. Bell passed by, Devin leaned in and in a low voice said, "I haven't told Keri about the bed-and-breakfast notion yet. Can we keep it between us for now?"

Ms. Bell's brows lifted, but she nodded. "My lips are sealed."

Inside, fairy lights cast everything in a soft, warm glow. Devin flashed to the last time they'd been there. Ms. Bell's reading, and her subsequent heart attack. A chill ran up her spine despite how warm the room was.

As if reading her mind, Ms. Bell turned to her. "It won't be like last time. I promise."

Devin smiled. "I know. You're doing great now."

Keri wandered ahead to greet Chris and Bill, and Devin watched her for a moment. She felt the pull to follow, but stood there, taking her in.

Ms. Bell lingered beside her, tilting her head to study her. "She's a good reason to stay."

Devin glanced over at Keri perusing a table of new releases. She looked up and smiled, tilting her head as if asking Devin to join her.

Yeah, Devin thought. She's worth staying for. She smiled back and walked up next to her.

Keri took her hand. "Let's get a glass of wine and find seats up front."

Jen Lyon read several excerpts from her new book, then took questions from the audience. After Jen had answered the last one, Chris stepped to the microphone. "Thank you all for coming. If you'd like to purchase books or get them signed, Jen will be at the table near the front."

Keri leaned in. Her voice tickled Devin's ear. "I'm going to grab a book. Meet me in line?"

"Sure. I'll get us another glass of wine," Devin said, watching Keri head toward the display.

At the bar, Devin waited in line behind a woman with short, black hair and a tailored blazer. She ordered a glass of wine, then turned to Devin, smiling. "Hi. I'm Lauren," she said, holding out her hand.

"Devin," she answered, shaking the woman's hand.

"Do you live here?" Lauren asked.

"No, but I grew up here."

The woman picked up the glass of wine placed on the bar in front of her. "Nice place to grow up?"

Devin nodded. Until it wasn't, she thought to herself. "Do you live here?"

"No. Cambria. I was in town showing a house. Saw a poster for the event and decided to come."

"You're a realtor?"

Lauren nodded. "Are you interested in buying something?"

Devin's heart skipped. "Actually…that empty storefront next door."

"I can arrange for you to take a look." Lauren reached into the pocket of her blazer and pulled out a business card. "Call me and we'll set up a time." Lauren smiled and walked away.

Devin stepped up to the makeshift bar. Bill stood behind it, a huge grin on his face. "Did you enjoy the reading?"

"Are you kidding? She's amazing."

Bill nodded. "One red, one white?" he asked pointing at the bottles of wine.

"Yes, please."

He placed two glasses of wine before her. She thanked him and headed back to Keri.

"Here you go." She handed a glass to Keri.

"Who was that?" Keri asked, nodding to Lauren. Her voice was light but her expression uncertain.

"A realtor," Devin said, keeping her voice even.

Keri frowned and opened her mouth to say something, but before she had the chance, the line inched forward, and it was their turn to meet the author.

Devin swallowed down whatever explanation wanted to come out. Not yet, she told herself. Not until she was absolutely sure and the timing was right.

Just as they finished getting their books signed and turned to leave, the front door flew open, overturning a nearby table of books. Tracy stumbled in, her face flushed and eyes wild. She reeked of alcohol. Her eyes darted around the room, then focused on Keri.

"You bitch," she slurred, lunging at Keri with both hands. Keri stumbled back, the book tumbling from her hand, her wineglass shattering as it hit the floor. Tracy shoved her again, harder the second time. Keri, already off balance, fell backward, her arm landing on a jagged piece of glass, and blood poured out.

Devin grabbed Tracy, as Chris hurried over with a clean towel, pressing it against the gash in Keri's arm. Tracy fought like a wild animal. She was out of control. She swung, landing a punch to Devin's mouth that sent pain blooming through her lip. Someone yelled at Tracy to stop. People backed away. Others stood frozen in place. Tracy lunged again, screaming curses. Jen Lyon rushed over, helping Devin wrestle Tracy onto her stomach. Once down, Jen sat on Tracy's back, keeping her pinned to the floor.

"Devin, I've got this," Jen Lyon said. "You go look after your girlfriend."

Even with Jen sitting on top of her, Tracy continued to struggle, reluctant to surrender, a stream of curses flying from her mouth.

Ms. Bell, calm but efficient, was holding her phone. "I've called the police," she announced in her authoritative teacher voice.

With Tracy restrained, Devin scrambled to Keri's side, her heart pounding and blood dripping down her chin. She looked at Keri, whose face was pale. "I'm so sorry," Devin whispered.

Keri reached out with her other arm and cupped her cheek. "This is not your fault."

"But it is."

Bill knelt next to Devin and handed her a handkerchief. "Here," he said.

Devin blinked, not understanding.

He pointed to her lip. "You're bleeding."

She touched her lip, then looked at her fingers. A look of surprise crossed her face. She pressed the handkerchief against her lip, wincing. "Thanks, Bill."

Jen, still sitting on Tracy's back, let out a sharp, frustrated huff. Tracy hadn't stopped screaming the whole time. "For God's sake, shut up!" Jen barked. When Tracy didn't, Jen's eyes narrowed. "If you don't, I swear I'll have Chris get me a towel to shove in your mouth." The room fell into a stunned silence for half a second before Tracy spat out something incoherent and gave another wild thrash.

A voice cut through the noise like a knife. "What the hell happened here?" Miranda strode into the bookstore. She scanned the room, taking in the shattered wineglass, the overturned table, the blood, Jen holding Tracy down, and then Devin and Keri on the floor. She knelt beside Keri. "Are you okay?"

"Yes, I'll be fine," Keri assured her.

Miranda glared at Devin. "What the hell happened?"

Devin swallowed hard, her lip throbbing. She tried to get to her feet, but her legs were shaky. "Tracy came out of nowhere. She attacked Keri," she said. "She's very drunk. I tried to stop her, but she..." Devin gestured to her mouth, the handkerchief now stained red.

Miranda's jaw tightened, and she nodded once. She stood and turned to Tracy, who still squirmed under Jen. "Tracy Miller, you're under arrest for assault, felony vandalism, and violating a restraining order. And that's just for starters." She gestured to the two uniformed officers near the door. "Cuff her."

"Devin, please—" Tracy screeched.

The officers moved in and cuffed Tracy's hands behind her back.

"Devin don't let them take me. Devin, please," Tracy wailed.

Miranda turned back to Keri. "Do you need an ambulance?"

Keri shook her head as Devin helped her to her feet. "No," she said.

"I'll take her to urgent care. It's still open," Devin said.

Miranda glared at Devin, then turned to the crowd. "My officers will need to take statements from everyone. Please don't leave until you've done that." She looked at Keri. "You two come by the station in the morning and I'll have someone take your statements then." With that, she strode out the door, the cuffed Tracy in tow.

The room buzzed with nervous energy. Two officers began taking statements. While they waited their turn, they congregated in small groups. More than a few were on their phones, calling and posting to social media.

Devin and Keri turned to Chris and Jen. "Jen, I'm so sorry," Devin said, holding the handkerchief to her lip. "Thanks for the assist."

"You're welcome." Jen shrugged. "Compared to the half-ton horses I train she was easy. But seriously, that woman needs some serious help. Who is she?"

Devin cringed. "My ex. It's a long story."

"I'll bet it's a good one," Jen said, one eyebrow raised.

Devin managed a weak chuckle. "You have no idea." She turned to Chris. "Do you need help cleaning this up?"

Chris shook his head. "No. You get Keri to urgent care. That arm needs stitches." He pointed to Devin's lip. "And you should have that looked at."

Devin hesitated for a second, then nodded. "All right. Thanks." She turned to Jen. "I'm sorry she ruined your book signing. But it was wonderful meeting you."

Jen smiled. "No problem—material for my next book," she said, half joking.

"I hope it's a bestseller," Devin said as she slipped an arm around Keri's waist. "Let's get you patched up." Keri nodded and leaned into Devin's embrace. After hugging Ms. Bell they stepped out onto the sidewalk, leaving the bookstore, and Tracy's rage, behind.

There were two people waiting at the urgent care office when they arrived. Keri's injury wasn't as serious as the others, so they waited almost an hour to be seen. The physician's assistant thoroughly cleaned the wound. It took five stitches to close. The doctor also examined Devin's lip, but decided stitching wasn't necessary.

It was close to midnight when they crossed the parking lot and Devin helped Keri into the Jeep. "Let's get you home," she said.

Keri nodded and tried to smile, but it didn't reach her eyes. "Will you stay?" Keri asked.

Devin leaned over and kissed her. "You couldn't get rid of me if you tried."

CHAPTER THIRTY-TWO

The sunlight crept through the curtains as Devin eased out of bed, careful not to wake Keri. She could tell by Keri's frown, even in sleep, that her arm still hurt more than she'd admitted.

Dressed in the same clothes she'd worn the night before, she padded into the kitchen, running a hand through her tangled hair. Moving on autopilot, she set up the coffee maker. She poured a cup and took a long sip, careful not to press too hard against her throbbing lip. The caffeine didn't quite chase away the exhaustion, but it helped.

She sat at the kitchen table and looked at her phone. It was time to let go of the past and move on. She needed to meet with HR. She also needed to figure out what came next for her—even if she wasn't sure what that meant for her and Keri.

She quickly searched for one-way flights to the Oakland Airport. There was one early tomorrow morning, and there was one seat left. She stared at the flight, her thumb hovering over the screen. She wasn't sure what she wanted anymore. Returning to the police department felt like stepping into a life that didn't fit now—but walking away from a career she'd loved didn't sit well either. Not wanting to overthink it—she could do that en route—she booked the flight.

The sound of soft footsteps pulled her out of her head. She looked up to see Keri shuffling into the kitchen, her hair mussed and dark circles under her eyes. She was wearing an old sweatshirt and a pair of flannel pajama pants, and she looked exhausted.

"Morning," Devin said, setting her phone down. She grabbed another mug and poured Keri a cup of coffee. "How's the arm?"

Keri shrugged, cradling the warm mug between her hands. "Hurts a little."

Devin didn't buy that for a second. The pinched look around Keri's eyes told her it hurt more than a little. After a long pause, Devin sat down across from Keri. "I, uh...I need to go to Haywood. I have to meet with HR tomorrow."

Keri stared at her, her eyes wide, her brow furrowed. "Are you going back to the department?"

Devin's stomach knotted. "I'm not a hundred percent sure yet. I want to hear what they have to say."

Keri stared at her, her expression unreadable. "When will you be back?"

Devin exhaled slowly, looking down at her coffee. "I don't know. Maybe a few days."

A deep crease formed between Keri's eyes. "You are coming back, right? You're not going to walk away again are you?"

Devin hated the uncertainty in her voice, and the way her chest tightened at the question. She forced a half-smile, trying to keep her voice light. "There are some things I need to take care of. Regardless of whether I stay in Haywood or come back here."

Keri remained silent but her hurt was obvious. Devin hated being evasive, but she couldn't make promises. Not yet.

Keri's eyes bore into Devin's, but she didn't say anything.

Devin set her cup down and knelt in front of Keri, wrapping her arms around her, holding her tight. Keri leaned into the hug, her voice muffled against Devin's shoulder. "I'll miss you."

Devin pressed a kiss to Keri's cheek before pulling back. "I'll miss you too."

CHAPTER THIRTY-THREE

At eleven o'clock Monday morning Devin squared her shoulders and walked into the Haywood Police Department. She carried a box containing her uniforms, service weapon, various pieces of equipment, and her badge. She'd entered the HR director's office and set the box on the desk. The woman leaned her head to the side. "What's this?"

Devin explained and handed her an envelope. Inside was her letter of resignation. "I've decided not to come back. I'm resigning."

Devin thought the woman looked relieved. She knew they viewed her as a liability, a reminder of a scandal they wanted buried. Her decision was best for both her and the department. But the decision had been hers, not theirs.

An hour, and many signatures later, she walked out of the building for the last time and into the warm noonday sun. She stood there on the sidewalk, squinting against the light, staring at the place she once called home, the place where she'd been proud to wear the uniform. It no longer felt that way.

Now officially unemployed, she squared her shoulders and called for an Uber.

She gave the driver the address of the U-Haul lot near her storage unit. Today was as good a day as any to clear it out.

The ride was quiet. They passed by familiar buildings and landmarks—her favorite burger joint, a Chinese restaurant, the park where she liked to run, and the gym where she'd worked out five days a week until she'd been shot. Her thoughts drifted back to Keri. She had texted her when she landed this morning just to let her know she'd gotten there safely. But Keri hadn't replied.

The U-Haul lot was mostly empty. She rented a truck with a ramp and took the keys from the man behind the counter. He only briefly looked away from the baseball game on the television mounted on the wall.

She drove the short distance to her storage unit, a ten-by-ten metal box stuffed with the remnants of her old life. She unlocked it and lifted the metal door. Dust mites and stale air hit her in the face. Everything she owned, other than her Jeep, was in there. A dozen boxes stacked on one side, a couple of plastic bins, a couch, recliner, small table and four chairs. In the very back, her queen-size mattress and bed frame.

She took a deep breath before attaching the metal ramp to the back of the truck. She pushed the couch up the ramp, her upper arm screaming in protest. She returned for the recliner, then the table and chairs. The mattress would go in last.

Piece by piece, box by box, her past life made the short journey from the unit to the truck. It wasn't until she reached the last box tucked in the back corner that she hesitated. She knew what was inside. A framed picture of her in dress uniform and the Medal of Valor awarded three years ago after pulling a child out of a burning building.

She opened the box and sank onto the concrete floor in a heap. She could still hear the applause from that day—her grandparents sitting in the audience, the way her heart had swelled with pride when the chief of police shook her hand and handed her the medal. It felt like a lifetime ago.

It wasn't until a tear splattered onto the box that she realized she was crying. She swiped her face with her sleeve and closed the box. The contents would stay packed away. It wasn't who she was anymore.

It was almost dark when she finished emptying the unit. Too exhausted to start the four-hour drive back to Morro Harbor, she drove the U-Haul to the Holiday Inn down the street. She'd get a fresh start in the morning.

The hotel room was dark when Devin woke to an alarm. For a moment, she wasn't sure where she was. Then it all came back—Haywood, HR, the storage unit.

She didn't waste time. She threw back the covers and climbed out of bed, eager to get on the road. She looked at herself in the bathroom mirror. The woman staring back looked like she'd been put through the ringer. She'd fallen asleep without eating or showering. The sweat and dust from the storage unit still clung to her skin. The heat of the shower washed over her, soothing her aching muscles and clearing the fog from her head.

Dressed and feeling slightly more human, Devin made her way downstairs. The desk clerk didn't look up from his phone when she entered the empty lobby. She hurried to the coffee bar and poured coffee into a to-go cup. The first sip burned her tongue, but it didn't deter her. She needed the jolt of caffeine to get her moving.

After leaving her key at the front desk, she grabbed a banana and donut and walked out the front door. The sun was just beginning to crawl over the hills and there was a chill in the early-morning air that was invigorating. She climbed into the U-Haul and pulled out of the parking lot. As she took the on-ramp for 92 South she smiled to herself.

She was going home.

The freeway stretched ahead of her, endless miles of pavement cutting through endless miles of farmland. Her phone sat on the passenger seat, the screen dark. She wished she'd called Keri last night to let her know what was going on, but she'd passed out the second she had lain down on the bed. It was too early to call now. Keri would still be asleep.

Devin stared at the road ahead, the sun teasing the horizon. Four hours. Four hours, and she'd be back in Morro Harbor. Back with Keri.

As the miles rolled on, and the sun rose higher, she smiled. For the first time in a very long time, she looked forward to what the future held.

It was a little after ten a.m. when she hit Morro Harbor City Limits. The familiar coastline felt like a welcoming embrace. She stopped in front of her father's house—her house now—and backed the U-Haul into the driveway. Her head fell back against the seat. She was home.

Pulling out her phone, she scrolled to Wren's number. It rang twice before she answered.

"Hi. What's up?" Wren asked.

"Do you have time to help me unload a truck?"

"A truck?"

"A U-Haul truck."

"Sure. Give me thirty."

While she waited she called Frank.

"Hi, Devin. What's up?"

She admired the lone egret that glided overhead. "I've decided what to do with Dad's boat," she said, a smile spreading across her face.

"Okay, what did you decide?"

"It's yours," she said. "Dad would want you to have it."

She was met with silence on the other end. "Frank? Are you there?"

She heard him blow out a breath. "I'm here."

She waited for him to continue.

"Devin, you can't just give me the boat. I'd love to have it, but you have to let me pay you for it."

"Absolutely not."

Seconds ticked by before Frank spoke. "All right, how about I make a donation to the Fisherman's Fund in Patrick's name?"

"I think he'd like that," Devin said, as Wren pulled up in front of the house. "How about I meet you at the dock later in the week and I'll give you the keys."

As she said goodbye, Wren climbed out of her car, balancing two steaming cups of coffee in a cardboard tray. Devin smiled, but her grin faltered when she spotted the man trailing behind her—Bo, holding a third cup of coffee.

"Bo?" Devin blinked in surprise.

"Hi," he said, sounding unsure if he was welcome.

Wren shrugged and smiled. "He can't lift much, but I brought him anyway."

Devin smiled and swallowed the lump in her throat.

Wren handed her a coffee. "Okay, put us to work."

"Let's put everything in the garage. I want to paint before I move in," Devin said opening the back of the U-Haul.

They got to work unloading the truck. The mattress was awkward. Bo stood back offering advice as Devin and Wren wrangled it into the garage. When Wren and Bo went back to retrieve boxes, Devin stepped aside and pulled out her phone to call Keri. It rang a half dozen times, but no answer. She swallowed her disappointment and left a message.

"Hey, it's me. I'm at my dad's house. If you're free, can you come by? We need to talk." She disconnected and returned to the truck to help Bo who was struggling to pick up a box with his good arm. Neither of them said anything, but the silence between them wasn't uncomfortable. It wasn't exactly easy, but it wasn't angry either.

By the time they had emptied the U-Haul, Devin's body ached, and exhaustion clawed at her. She leaned against her father's pickup. Wren stretched her back and smiled at Devin.

"What are you going to do with the truck?"

Devin turned around and looked at the small, beat-up truck and smiled. "I think I'll keep it. It's perfect for hauling a kayak around."

Wren grinned. "I guess this means you're staying."

Devin looked at Bo, then back at Wren. "Yes. I'm staying."

"Good," was all she said.

Devin nodded. "Thanks for helping. I owe you both."

"Anytime." Wren smiled. "That's what friends are for."

Devin glanced at Bo. "Thank you."

He nodded. "You're welcome," he said, then nodded to Wren's car. "Let's go, I'm starving."

"Okay, bro, let's go."

Devin watched them pull away, Bo sitting in the passenger seat. The sight of him, sober, not enraged, felt like another piece of the past settled into place. She smiled as she walked across the dirt yard and began pulling Mrs. Booker's trash can to the curb. Now that she was staying, she'd need to spruce up the front of the house, maybe plant a few gardenias. She'd have to ask her grandfather if he could help with that.

As she set Mrs. Booker's second can at the curb, Keri's car rounded the corner and Devin's heart jumped to her throat.

Keri pulled into the space Wren had vacated and stepped out, and with eyes wide, looked from the U-Haul to Devin. "What's going on?" Keri's voice was cautious, but hopeful.

Devin didn't answer. Instead, she crossed the yard in a few quick strides and wrapped her arms around Keri. "I'm home."

EPILOGUE

Devin arrived early and pulled into the same parking space at Harbor Beach she'd pulled into a year ago. So much had happened in that year.

Bo had been sober for eleven months, and they were working on strengthening their fragile friendship. He'd started seeing a therapist and continued to attend AA meetings. He wouldn't get his license back for another two months and Devin had continued to drive him on Wednesdays. If he successfully completed his two years of probation he could petition the court to have the felony charge reduced to a misdemeanor.

Devin had also started seeing a therapist and was better able to put Melissa's death into perspective. Through therapy she'd let go of the guilt that had plagued her for over a decade. She was still working on forgiving her father, but she had anchored herself in Morro Harbor, something a year ago she was sure she would never do.

The Melissa Bailey Bed-and-Breakfast was up and running and rooms were booked out for the next six months.

Devin had finished renovating her father's—strike that—her house, and Keri would be moving in soon. Keri had offered Wren the apartment over the wine bar and Wren had eagerly accepted.

Leasing the vacant space between Rainbow Books and Wine Time seemed impulsive at the time, but now Morro Harbor Kayak, Paddleboard, and Surf Shop was thriving. Hiring Wren to run it had worked out well for both of them. The arrangement allowed Wren to work and attend school and gave Devin the time to work on her house and help at the bed-and-breakfast when needed. Even more unexpectedly, Devin was surfing again. The first time she paddled out past the break, her hands shook, but the ocean welcomed her back like an old friend. Wren had even talked her and Bo into teaching her how to surf.

Perhaps the most unexpected change of all was Miranda. She had started dating a sociology professor who had recently moved to Morro Harbor. Her dislike of Devin had evaporated overnight, and she'd offered Devin a part-time position as the high school liaison officer. The job was nothing like the policing she'd done before, but helping kids navigate the obstacles between adolescence and adulthood gave her a purpose she didn't know she needed.

And now, here she was, on the precipice of something else she hadn't expected but wanted more than anything. She'd asked Keri to marry her, and Keri had said yes.

Thus, the reason for her being at the beach today. It was their wedding day. There was never a doubt that they'd be married on the beach where they'd spent so much of their youth.

Devin climbed out of her Jeep and pulled out the bright-pink surfboard. Bo was bringing Melissa's. The two boards would stand upright in the sand behind Frank, who would be officiating the ceremony. It was Keri's idea, a way to have a piece of Melissa present.

She carried the board down the small dune, the sand shifting beneath her feet. Wren, Chris, and Bill were already there, setting up the small wooden arch that would frame the ocean behind them. Chris shot her a grin. "You ready for this?"

A smile spread across Devin's face. "More than ready."

Wren wiggled her eyebrows. "You gonna cry?"

"Of course not," Devin said, but Wren's smirk told her that no one believed her.

Chris chuckled. "Uh-huh. Sure. I'll have tissues ready."

Devin rolled her eyes but couldn't stop the grin tugging at her lips. The last year had changed her in so many ways, and yet, at this moment, she felt more like herself than she had in years.

Bo arrived with his parents and walked across the sand carrying Melissa's pink board under his arm. Their eyes met. Neither of them said anything. They didn't need to. He stood the board in the sand next to Devin's, then stepped back, letting the moment settle between them.

As the final preparations came together, guests started arriving, barefoot and smiling, the salty air buzzing with quiet excitement. Devin fingered the charm on her mother's necklace, her heart hammered as the reality of the day sank in.

Before she knew it, a friend of Bo's started playing the wedding march on a guitar, and everyone stood.

Dressed in white pants, a white shirt, and barefoot, Devin stood next to her grandfather. He looked down at her and smiled. "Ready?" he asked.

She nodded, and they started down the makeshift aisle together. As they walked toward Frank, she spotted Ms. Bell behind her grandmother, dabbing her eyes with a tissue. Devin breathed deeply, the weight of the moment settling in the best possible way.

When she reached the front, her grandfather kissed her on the cheek and took his seat next to her grandmother. She took her place next to Wren, her best person, and smiled at Frank. When she turned around, Keri, dressed in a simple yet elegant white dress, her hair loose and sun-kissed, was walking down the aisle holding onto her father's arm, his expression a mix of pride and emotion. Devin's throat tightened at the sight. She swore she could hear the ocean hush for just a moment, as if it too was pausing to take her in.

When they reached the front, Keri's father kissed her on the cheek and sat down next to her mother. Keri turned to Devin and smiled, and the last of Devin's nerves faded away.

"Hi," Keri whispered.

Devin took her hands, Keri's touch grounding her. "Hi."

Frank cleared his throat and smiled at them. "I think that's my cue."

Laughter rippled through the small crowd, and the ceremony began. As she spoke her vows and listened to Keri recite hers, Devin knew with absolute certainty that she was exactly where she was meant to be. As the sun dipped lower in the sky, she kissed her wife for the first time.

Her life had come full circle. She'd returned to Morro Harbor a year ago, haunted by guilt and chased by ghosts. Today, she stood on the same sand, surrounded by love, knowing that she had found her way home.

Bella Books
Happy Endings Live Here
P.O. Box 10543
Tallahassee, FL 32302
Phone: (800) 729-4992
BellaBooks.com

More Titles from Bella Books

Jones – Gerri Hill
978-1-64247-598-2 | 260 pages | Mystery
One weekend getaway, six friends, and a deadly secret that will wash
away everything they thought they knew.

Merry Weihnachten – E. J. Noyes
978-1-64247-610-1 | 292 pages | Romance
Christmas traditions aren't the only things getting mixed up when
these two hearts collide beneath the mistletoe.

Sweet Home Alabarden Park – TJ O'Shea
978-1-64247-570-8 | 362 pages | Romance
She came to restore a royal estate—she never expected to rebuild her
heart.

Dr. Margaret Morgan – Christy Hadfield
978-1-64247-628-6 | 286 pages | Romance
Facing the professor on campus everyone hates is terrifying—but
falling for her might be even worse.

Overtime – Tracey Richardson
978-1-64247-630-9 | 278 pages | Romance
A charming romance about second chances, found family, and scoring
the goal that matters most.

The Big Guilt – Renée J. Lukas
978-1-64247-657-6 | 206 pages | Romance
What if the one who got away became the one you can't have?

www.ingramcontent.com/pod-product-compliance
Lightning Source LLC
Chambersburg PA
CBHW020632110726
47899CB00002B/739